THE BETRAYAL

STACY TOWNEND

Copyright notice

Townend ST

The Betrayal, A Mercian Tale, A Historical Fiction Circa 757-796
Copyright 2022, Townend ST Amazon Edition
All characters and events in this publication, other than those clearly in the public domain, are fictitious and any resemblance to actual persons, living or dead, is purely coincidental.

ALL RIGHTS RESERVED. No part of this publication may be reproduced, stored in a retrieval system, or transmitted in any other form or by any other means without the prior written permission of the author, nor be otherwise circulated in any form of binding or cover other than that in which it is published and without a similar condition being imposed on the subsequent buyers.

Cover design by

Stacy T Townend

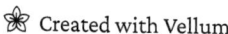 Created with Vellum

CONTENTS

Character List	7
1. The Treachery	11
2. The Killing	23
3. The Devastation	32
4. The Plan	42
5. The Trip	50
6. The Meeting	56
7. The Deaths	63
8. The King's Meeting	70
9. The Training	78
10. The Attack	86
11. The Search for the King	93
12. The King is saved	100
13. The Death	107
14. The Honour	114
15. The kidnap	121
16. The Rescue	129
17. The Traitor Lavos	138
18. The Traitor Sigmund	143
19. The Enemy	151
20. The Betrayal	159
21. The Fight for Farndon	166
22. The Retreat	174
23. The Slaughter	181
24. The Chase	189
25. The Aftermath	198
26. The Future	204

Author Notes	211
About the Author	213
Acknowledgments	215
The Revenge	217

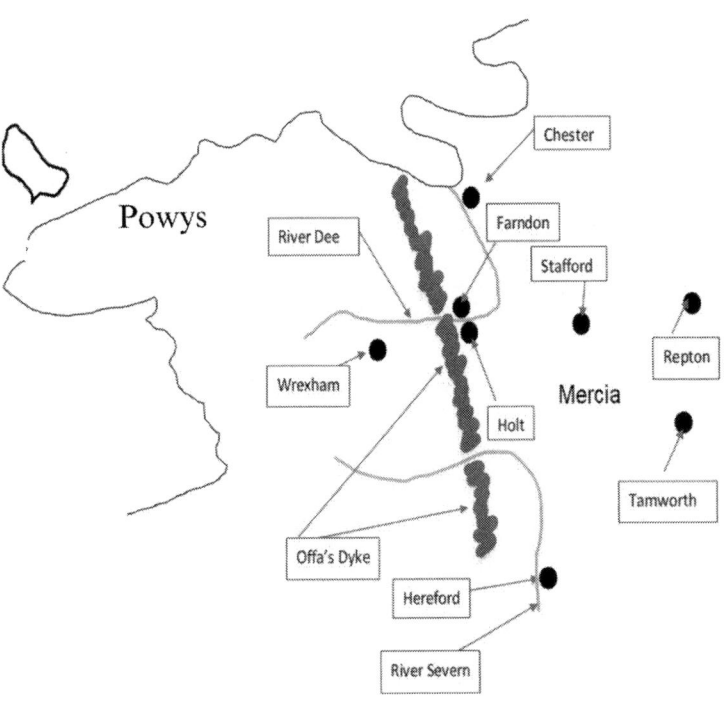

CHARACTER LIST

King Offa 757_796
  Oswi young proven warrior of King Offa and youngest son of Ludeca Ealdorman of Offa
    Ludeca Ealdorman under King Offa
    Sigmund Ealdorman under King Offa
    Alestan Ealdorman under King Offa
    Harrick Senior Warrior to Ealdorman Sigmund
    Mord (The Hound) Captain of Sigmund
    Hern
    Ludic
    Wulfure warriors of Ealdorman Ludeca
    Bern an old warrior who served under Ludeca and trained Oswi
    Alfe
    Bergad
    Brune
    Egbert
    Ethelbert
    Edhert
    Ren

Strum
Dristan
Thornstan
Wigstan
Winebert warriors training under Oswi & Bern
Ceoal Squire to Oswi
Raffe Squire to Bern
Shia wife to Bern
Drax eldest son of Bern

Thane Eldrig
　Eleen daughter to Eldrig
　Lavos Captain of Eldrig
　Raulf – former Section Leader
　Trevik
　Alun all old warriors of Eldrig
　Lud
　Beorn
　Cernwulf
　Thornhed
　Wigson warriors and supporters of Lavos

Brak Smith to Eldrig
　Brak Son of Brak the smith, warrior, and hunter
　Gava Butcher to Eldrig
　Atal son of Gava
　Hardison & Loff twins and Hunters for the village of Eldrig
　Aruth - Section leader
　Ceolstan
　Thrun
　Wareson Loyal warriors of Eldrig
　Ethane elderly maid to Eleen
　Rolf Steward of Eldrig

The Raiders

Jarl Bjorn leader of four ships crews who harass Eldrig's village
- Freda wife to Bjorn
- Healfden warrior son of Bjorn (and Captain)
- Orm Steersman of Roar (fame and spear)
- Gudrun Seer, healer of Bjorn
- Gorm a captain of Bjorn
- Renkel a captain of Bjorn
- Frode a captain of Bjorn
- Arn
- Bo
- Berg 3 warrior friends of Healfden
- Rune a scout (older brother to Berg)
- Tove senior scout
- Svend a scout

Other Characters

Manse The Merchant
- Acel
- Frode two hunter friends of Brak the smith's son
- Frik an old woodsman
- Frey his wife and healer
- Drom a warrior
- Lan a warrior

Bledri Tribal Chief of Powy's
- Rathan, Chief Warrior of Bledri

CHAPTER 1
THE TREACHERY

T he clouds slowly rolled in as the autumn sky darkened. No stars shone through, and the moon was a slim crescent giving off only a small shimmer of light. The band of warriors had been sent to track a group of raiders who'd attacked three nights ago. The raiders had burned down farms and slain families before stealing food and livestock. It hadn't been the first such attack.

Eldrig the thane had tasked his captain and guards to find and kill the band of raiders that had been troubling the area these past months. The captain was unhappy at being ordered to chase the raiders down. He knew as there'd been no survivors from the attack that these were no mere raiders, but seasoned warriors looking to gain wealth and land. He didn't want to be killed out in the wilds fighting for his weak thane.

It had started with the odd small attack by a small group of raiders stealing sheep and cattle or emptying a barn of food, this had been going on some time now through the early spring and long summer months. Then the rapes and sometimes murders started, and though only a few people were killed it was worrying. Thane

Eldrig was troubled, and his people came to him to demand action and justice. Eldrig had ruled over the small walled village of Farndon and the surrounding fertile lands for years. There'd been trouble and strife from his neighbouring thanes, Ealdorman, and raiders from across the river that divided his land from that of the kingdom of Powys, but this was completely different.

Thane Eldrig was angry, annoyed, and upset with the current situation; the small number of deaths, of stolen cattle, and the quantity of winter stores being emptied had risen sharply during the last month. He'd spent money arranging for extra men to guard against the raiders, these men searched for the attackers though always returned unsuccessful having never found them. He was furious as some of these craven men had even deserted their posts after taking wages from him.

The most recent attack on the small settlement of Crag Rock had been the last straw. Not only was Crag Rock the most fertile of his lands and the producer of the largest stores of grain, but it also provided fish and eels from the fish traps and boasted the best hunters. They added deer, rabbits, birds, and the occasional boar to support the village and surrounding area. What irked Thane Eldrig most was that Crag Rock had provided a long line of steadfast, strong, loyal warriors who'd served him, his father and grandfather, and generations before. While Eldrig's family had ruled the area, the senior men of the family of Crag Rock had served and fought for them. This was no way for that loyalty to be repaid.

Thane Eldrig would have acted at this point anyway, even if he'd not been visited by the Elder of Crag Rock. He'd been left with no choice but to do something to counter the raids.

So now, with the latest attack still fresh in the minds of his people and warriors, Thane Eldrig demanded action from his captain, sending him out with a group of his household warriors and a few old hunters to seek and destroy the raiders. Eldrig had known this would be no easy task for his captain and men, but they needed to respond.

The dozen warriors and their captain had spent the last hours of daylight tracking the raiders but had no success in locating them. As the shadows lengthened, the captain called out for his men to stop and make camp for the night. The chosen site was in the shelter of a small wood. As the group settled down to cook the birds and rabbits trapped earlier that day, the sun slowly set behind the tall trees the sky darkening as night fell, and the heat from the sun soon dispersed leaving a slight chill to the evening air. The captain, a cruel hard man, looked around the camp to choose the sentries for the night. He'd never allocate the duty to his chosen friends or volunteer himself, but he knew and had planned who would perform the onerous duty.

The three older warriors chosen for sentry duty strode to the edge of the camp, hands clasping swords and axes. The senior of the three, Raulf, spoke quietly to his companions.

"Well, lads, nothing fucking new. Sentry duty again and I can guarantee we'll be stood here half the night if not all of it."

Trevik's answering laughter sounded like a bear growling, deep guttural, and loud. "The captain and young ones can't keep up with the likes of us seasoned warriors. They need their beauty sleep."

Alun chuckled darkly. "Blooming seasoned. Don't make me laugh, long in the tooth you mean. Come on, you got up three times last night, Trevik, to take a piss, and that's only the times you woke me."

The three men laughed as they reached the trees, a short distance from the camp.

Raulf looked at his two loyal friends. For twenty-five years, he'd served the current thane, Eldrig, and that didn't include the seven previous years for his father. Cernherd. His two friends had performed similar service to Raulf.

Originally, Raulf had eleven men under his direct command, a mix of archers and swordsmen, and he'd been second to the old captain, Rhernhard. Rhernhard had been Raulf's uncle and had passed away many moons ago from wounds taken in a battle against the bloody Welsh. Now Raulf stood in the trees with his two remaining men, loyal friends, and true comrades in arms, Trevik once as strong and ugly as any growling bear in the forest, and Alun fast, sleek, and agile like a fox hunting. Alun had once been the finest shot with a bow or knife, but that honour now went to another, Aruth a young section leader of Thane Eldrig's. Aruth had followed Alun around from a young age watching and mimicking him until Alun decided to tutor him.

Raulf sighed, remembering how many times they'd risked their lives fighting for the father and son thanes against the raiders and other local thanes and lords. All three had stepped down from adventures such as this long ago. Normally, they'd stick to patrolling the village walls or standing guard against the Welsh at the broken-down watchtower across the river Dee. The recent attack at Crag Rock had hit Raulf hard. The settlement was both his birthplace and where he'd been raised. The settlement had been managed and worked by his family for generations.

He was the Elder, following his uncle Rhernhard's death. All of the families killed in the latest attack had been Raulf's kin. His uncle's family lost four male cousins and three women. Hence he and his two sworn men now stood on sentry duty, while searching for the latest attackers on a dark autumnal night.

Raulf's anger when he'd been summoned by the Thane from sentry duty across the river at the watchtower had Trevik and Alun fighting to hold Raulf down, pinning him as he raged on and on when they had arrived at Crag Rock to see first-hand the death and destruction the stench of burning and death hung heavy in the air like a dark veil. The friends had never seen him so angered and thirsty for bloody revenge.

Raulf had been most upset as his young niece of thirteen summers had been brutally and repeatedly raped by the attackers. She'd still been alive when Raulf had found her battered and bleeding. Her life had been slowly ebbing away due to the massive internal damage to her petite body. Sareen, Raulf's brave niece, had laid there dying, so small and fragile in her uncle's arms, as she'd slowly spoken, between sobs, the story of the attack and the rapes and murders. Raulf, Trevik, and Alun had all wept when her mind and body had finally given up. Raulf had held her body tight hugging her tight to his chest and kissing her blood-stained head.

Raulf had attended and spoken with Thane Eldrig. His grief had made him demand instant action from his Thane. Trevik and Alun had stood close by as Raulf calmly spoke with his Thane as he explained what he desired. Once the course of action had been decided, the trio of friends had simply turned, dressed for war, and followed Raulf as they'd always done. The bond of brotherhood of the warriors would not allow them any other course of action. They'd walk into the fiery depths of hell to follow each other if required.

It was a dark, quiet, still night as the three friends walked the camp's perimeter, changing direction and route at every pass of the circuit. Old hands such as they never strode the same path. You never knew who was out there watching from the shadows. The three of them hadn't lived the long years into their fifties without being careful and attentive to every detail and sound.

Raulf had just completed his circuit to turn and pass Alun, and then Trevik once more, when he heard a noise only just audible. He stopped. Instinct took over and he dropped to one knee sliding his seax from its belt and gripping it firmly. In his other hand, he held ready his small war axe.

What had he heard? Was it just his imagination taking over? Everywhere seemed quiet now. Too quiet. There was a deathly stillness in the darkness, and it just didn't feel right to his senses. Silently, he slowly inched forward, one slow, calm, measured step at a time. He was alert and listening for any sound.

He sensed Alun was dead before he found his body, the stench of blood, guts, and bowels overwhelming. Even after all these years, it made him gag. The foul smell of brutal death. Other bodies lay near Alun with arrows and knives protruding from them the light from the moon filtered through the trees casting shadows on the bodies it was only as he inspected each one he saw how Alun had dispatched them. They'd all died hard, the leaves and branches covered with warm sticky blood, Raulf had knelt in the blood of Alun as he knelt by his side.

Raulf sighed to himself, yet another friend lost in war. The raider scum. He'd kill the lot of them if Alun hadn't already done so. He bent down to look at Alun's face, reaching down with one hand to touch Alun's face and close the wide-open eyes.

"Rest easy, Alun. Trevik and I'll catch and bloody gut them and send them all back to hell." Raulf examined the dead bodies. Something wasn't right here. From the signs of attack, they'd come from inside the camp where the others should be sleeping. How strange. Surely, he'd have heard the camp come under attack. How had their enemy passed the three of them on sentry duty? They'd have had to be exceptional hunter-warriors to do so. The darkness of the trees and the debris of leaves and twigs strewn over the ground would have made it difficult to approach unheard.

Raulf looked around him once more before suddenly deciding to change direction. Raulf replaced his axe on his belt, keeping his seax in his hand as he crawled away from where Alun lay, taking a direct route across to the open camp area, hoping he'd reach Trevik so they could wake the sleeping warriors and captain. He could see the glow from the remains of the fire just off to the right and the boulders near to it where the captain and other warriors were resting. It was too dark with the waning moon to see clearly into the camp, but he could see the shapes of men huddled in blankets and the outline of the horses further back in the trees.

Slowly he crept onwards, inching his way through the long frosty grass. Stopping, and listening he heard no sounds, no snores, no breathing, just silence, a strange silence almost as if it was supernatural and forced. It wasn't just the silence but the feel of the darkness encompassing him. It didn't feel right at all. His mind went into overdrive. Had the men left, or were they dead in the blankets

THE BETRAYAL

around the dying embers of the fire? Where was Trevik? He should have seen his form moving through the trees even in the poor moonlight, as he walked behind the horses as part of his sentry duty. It was wrong. The situation felt all wrong. He stopped, waited, and listened once more. He was sure he wasn't alone but couldn't hear or see a threat. He stood now and drew his axe then slowly moved once more. He was nearly across the open area to the trees. A large, dark, twisted, burnt tree stood to his immediate left. He stepped in near silence forward once more, his heart pounding in his chest, rushing his blood around his body as in the old days of battle, his old limbs once more fuelled with power and strength.

A slight rustle of dried crisp leaves had him alert once more. He quietly stood, breathing calmly and slowly to control the anger, and rushing blood within him. He needed control of all his senses and the skills to combat the threat approaching him. He turned and stood in the darkness of the large, dark twisted tree; the campfire would be glowing behind him. He hoped this would help when the attack came as they could be slightly blinded by its glow. He calmly waited in the shadow of the tree. He watched as, from the darkness, appearing like horned and armed demons, four shadows grew and crept towards him. This was it. They were searching for him or Trevik or probably both. Time slowed. At that moment, he could see the slow, lumbering gait of the men as they drew closer to him. He controlled his breathing, calming his heart as if waiting to beat fast and hard when the attack eventually came.

He was sure they didn't see him or sense him. He saw the first man and moved to step from the tree's shelter to begin his attack. He held his axe high to take the man through the neck. But suddenly, a dark shape, shouting and growling, shot from the undergrowth, swinging his sword wildly. The first man ducked and spun to Trevik's left in a blur of movement, yet graceful and with speed like a dancer twirling around. Trevik took two more steps away from the warrior, half turning his face to look upon his killer. Abruptly, he fell to his knees, guts sliced open, quickly spilling over his belt and trousers. The gore ran onto his legs and the leafy grass in front of him.

Trevik looked up at the men. "Treacherous hounds from hell,' Trevik said as he made eye contact with his killer. A knife sliced quickly across his throat ending the proud warrior's life instantly, and Trevik's body dropped heavily to the floor.

It was then that Raulf stepped from the shadows of the tree, his face a mask of anger and upset. He stepped towards the four warriors, calm and content that he'd be reunited soon with his loyal friends.

"Hello, lads looking for me. It's time to tackle the old lion now. Let us dance."

A voice deep and dark responded. "Old lion. Don't make me laugh, more like a lame old dog more like. Let's get this finished once and for all."

"These three dog turds always thought themselves elite and better than the rest of us. We've proven them wrong now, chopped them down to size. What say you, men?"

Abruptly, more shapes stepped out from the darkness of the trees to surround him. Proud, Raulf, stood alone in defiance. The warriors rushed forward to throw a circle around him.

Raulf laughed, joyfully as thought to himself, no escape this time then? Controlling his breathing and emotions Raulf readied himself for the imminent attack. Then with a blur of speed as in his younger years, he spun, turned, jumped, twisted, and ducked as he danced around the swords, spears, and axes that reached out to end his life here in the trees.

He stabbed and swung both his seax and axe. The first of his enemies fell, his head exploding like some overripe fruit split by the axe. The second had his sword arm taken from the elbow, blood pumping everywhere as he bled out. Blades struck Raulf's body, cuts, and nicks on his arms and torso. He was tiring, each cut slowed him further. The blood flowing from his wounds sapped his strength. He took the last soul to join him on his journey, his seax stuck in the foeman's eye.

Raulf looked at his attackers. Why did the grinning idiot look so tall? It was then he realised he was lying on his back, dying, he saw the tall man lean over and look him straight into his eyes.

"Lavos you slimy turd,"

Raulf smiled to himself as his life slowly ebbed away. Once more, he saw the smiling face of Sareen as she played in the yard by the old barn. He saw his family and friends. He considered the dead raiders about him. He'd served out his justice. He was content.

THE SMALL WOOD was quiet once again, Lavos and his men stood looking at the bodies around them.

A raider arrived on horseback, the stallion a huge dark shape, snorting, and feet pounding the blood-soaked earth. The raider jumped down, snarling angrily, and grabbing at the tall man's throat with a huge hand who had been standing calmly cleaning the blood from his weapons. "What the Odin happened" he shouted. "Three old men you told me, three OLD MEN, old warriors we need out of the way." He spun around pointing his gleaming sword at the dead attackers. "I didn't expect to lose any of my men this night.'

'This dog,' he kicked Raulf's body, 'took three men as did the knife thrower. And the ugly-looking brute killed four warriors and wounded my son. He may yet lose sight in one eye." He took three steps away from Lavos and spun with a lethal speed, his sword in his hand strong and sure pointed at his throat. "I have ten dead men this night. The rewards you spoke of in our agreement had better be true and forthcoming you cur, or you'll join the dead yourself."

Lavos sighed, "It'll happen. The trap will be laid as promised." He turned away and called to his men. "Throw our guards' bodies across the horses. We'll return with them. It'll add to the terror and worry of our people, as planned. They need to know they're not safe in Farndon, and their Thane cannot protect them any longer."

The raider turned from Lavos and then climbed upon his dark wild horse pulling its head from the dead and leading his men into the darkness of the trees and away from the carnage of the recent battle.

The bodies of the three proud old warriors soon laid over their horses, who snorted and skittered, nervous of the smell of blood. They were led back to the camp, and the horses tethered for the night.

Lavos angrily spoke to his men, noticing the bodies close to the camp. "Tie the horses to those trees away from our camp. We'll stay here the rest of the night and start our journey home tomorrow." He turned, scowling at the path he'd chosen that night. He spoke once more to his men. "Thornhed and you too, Wigson, you two take the first watch. I don't trust that Viking raider scum. They may decide to come calling. STAY ALERT." He looked around the rest of the warriors. "No more ale tonight, lads. We sleep with our swords and axes close."

Turning from his men, he strode back to the campfire. Kneeling, he raked the embers and added more wood. He sat watching the flames, brooding; his face stern and his dark eyes looking deep into the flames. "Soon," he whispered to himself. "Soon bitch, you'll writhe, squirm, and scream under me. Soon very soon." A cruel smile crept upon the dark mask of his face as he thought of the pleasure and pain he could bring to the bitch that had rejected his every offer.

Once seated back on the rock with his cloak over him, he pondered his choice. For years he'd tried to gain the hand of his Thane's only daughter, hoping in time to become the thane of the area. The small old walled Roman village sat upon the river and his thane was wealthy from trading with merchants from across the seas. The people who lived within the village and surrounding farms lived comfortable lives. The land was fertile for crops, and herds of sheep and cattle lived on the nearby hills. The river provided food and transport.

It could all be his if he helped the raiders and killed his thane. He had gambled with the raiders, trusting that if he helped them to conquer this area by betraying his thane and people, he'd then rule it while the raiders continued to attack and claw their way further inland to take control of the kingdom of the Mercians. He dreamed of being Thane Lavos, and it had taken over every waking moment of his life. He should rule Farndon. Lavos did ponder at these dark times when it had not gone as planned if he'd made an error of judgment. Would the raiders even leave him alive after they had control of this swathe of land? He was now unsure as the village sat at a crucial point of the river and also had a bridge close by which a land army could use to smash further inland to the lush farmlands and villages. They might not even wait till the village had been conquered. Should he continue with the gamble or warn his lord and master? He sat quietly thinking while his warriors dealt with the dead.

He saw the body of Raulf and looked hard at the limp form of the old warrior. "Smug bastard," he said to no one in particular. The cruel smile once more spread across his face.

"Yes," he said to himself, it is the right decision. "I'm glad I got you Raulf, old boy, so very glad I got you out of the way now I can rule."

Wigson walked over to him. "Lavos the raider scum hasn't moved very far away. They're just along the ridge of trees at the next hill. Are we staying or moving on?" Lavos pondered for a quick moment before replying to his long-time friend and confident Wigson.

"We stay, but we keep alert, and change over guards regularly. We don't want to get caught out if they decide to sneak back and attack us."

He turned away clutching his cloak and wrapped it around him.

He'd not be standing duty tonight. He'd leave it for Wigson to organise as usual.

～

On the hill close by the raiders leader, Jarl Bjorn, stood looking across at the faint shapes and shadows of the group of supposed allies. He smiled to himself. He'd played this game of divide and conquer before. Wherever he went, be it against the Franks or the Picts. Whoever, there was always someone willing to betray the village or leader for money or in this case a woman.

Lavos was a weak man to betray his lord and master for a mere woman, even if she was the lord's daughter. He'd have just taken her and brutally raped her; had his pleasure then disposed of her. The lord would have been weakened by such an act, and he could have exploited it and taken control. He laughed loudly. Never mind. He could always kill his allies and have the daughter himself. Now that was a good plan.

He turned to his own men, " Do we have food? I need some food. Get it sorted, you bastards." Turning his back, he walked back into his camp, happy at the potential outcomes even though he'd lost men, good men, too, but well, it happened. It would just mean more money for those left alive. He walked towards his son to check how he was, he hoped that Healfden wouldn't lose the sight in his eye. If he did, then Healfden would have to be killed as he'd not be strong enough or quick enough to lead the warriors and eventually take his place as Jarl of the band of warriors. It would be a shame as Healfden showed promise as a leader.

CHAPTER 2
THE KILLING

Three nights earlier all was quiet within the group of four farm huts sheltered around a large communal barn. A small wooden fence surrounded the compound this was to keep the animals enclosed rather than a barrier to keep people out. The farming community sat near the river which had an irrigation channel leading from a small wooden sluice gate and ran through the middle of the fields to aid watering and crop production. The farm had its own deep well which naturally filled from the small springs providing fresh chilled water that ran through the rocks to the river. Nobody stirred within the confines of the huts the families all sleeping soundly they would not be rising for another few hours as they waited until just before dawn broke to rise and break their fast, then heading out to the fields and barns to tend the animals and harvest the fields to prepare them once again for planting next year's crops. The raiders had chosen to arrive by boat slowly, stealthy inching upstream the men rowing in almost silence the boat glided through the water. This was a small party of warriors only sixteen in total, though all seasoned, willing, and able to cause mayhem and destruction.

. . .

Jarl Bjorn stood on the prow with his eldest son Healfden a young proud warrior. Bjorn's steersman Orm stood at the steering helm of the boat Roar speaking to the warriors at the oars as he moved the boat around the rivers bends and away from the sharp rocks and reef-covered mudbanks. Orm had sailed this path before over the previous months the last time a week before as he and some of the men had played the part of merchants to allow them the freedom of the river and to get used to its navigation for this very deed. They had even managed to land at the small pier and walk the paths that ran to the small settlement they had arrived late one evening to check the area over once everyone would have returned home after the day's work.

The crew knew their job, all were experienced in sailing the meandering rivers and open seas. In near silence, the oars dipped into the river moving Roar along to reach its target gliding smoothly through the river. They along with Orm and Jarl Bjorn knew the point to land at the irrigation channels where the channel and sluice gate sat along the edge of the river bank a small broken-down pier sat, Orm had checked it over before and knew it was sound and strong enough to tie Roar up to it after the previous scouting trip. A small guard of two would be left aboard Roar just in case anyone passed close by or came to investigate. Quietly and slowly the crew pulled on the oars to inch Roar up the river. Orm leaned over and spoke quietly to Jarl Bjorn, "Around this curve and then after the next right bend you should be able to see the small pier, it is a dark night so you will need to keep alert Jarl we do not know want to miss it"

"Yes, Steersman I am aware" Jarl Bjorn sternly replied.

Orm turned and went back to the steering arm to keep Roar in the dark deeper flowing river. The dark night made navigation hard, Orm was so glad he had managed to sail the river a few times the last

THE BETRAYAL

week as he could see rocks and shallows and had drawn a small map to assist with guidance. Orm told the warriors at the oars to slow the pace as they neared the last right bend, Healfden stood on the prow and pointed to his right then waved his arm to advise Orm to slow the Roar down, "Gently men, nice and steady and no talking for now" said Orm to the men sat at the banks of oars.

Jarl Bjorn looked over to his son Healfden a questioning look on his face, Healfden turned and spoke quietly to his father in a whisper "Oars in father, we are almost at the pier"

Jarl Bjorn turned and stepped to the middle of the row of warriors and spoke "Oars in, let her glide to the pier now lads, Orm turn two points to the right, we should glide nice and smoothly against the pier"

" Yes, my lord" replied Orm. Roar glided silently the last few yards to the pier, like a sleek otter swimming in the dark water hunting. A slight bump was all that could be heard as Roar touched the pier instantly the two men who would guard Roar jumped off tying ropes to secure Roar to the pier. Jarl Bjorn stood looked at his men and stepped onto the pier, Healfden joined him and Orm had the warriors pass up his Lord's shield and helm before climbing to stand beside him. Jarl Bjorn waved his arm and strode off the pier as the remaining eleven warriors grabbed shields, helms, swords, and axes to follow their Jarl to take the war to the small community.

ORM ORGANISED the two men to stay and watch Roar putting them a short distance from the pier by an old oak tree, while he was doing this Jarl Bjorn sent out two warriors to check all was quiet.

JARL BJORN TURNED to his son Healfden "You will go with your three warriors and assist Frode and his men" Healfden turned to go " Healfden my son, take care and listen to Frode, no rash action."

"Yes, Father I understand."

Jarl Bjorn turned to Frode a long-standing friend and captain, "Take my son and his men, Orm and his second go down through the fields and down the far side of the sluice channel then circle around and come from the roadside and attack the buildings from that side"

"Yes Bjorn" Frode replied gruffly he was a childhood companion of Jarl Bjorn and one of the few men who called him by name without receiving a punch to his face for lack of respect.

Frode turned to Healfden, Orm, and the others "Come, quickly and be quiet, we can't be heard by the families, come now we need to move fast" With that he set off at a steady jog, Healfden and Orm quickly followed in his wake with the rest of the men picking up shields having to run hard to catch up with Frode.

Jarl Bjorn then waved his arm at the remaining warriors to follow him. He set off through the fields with the warriors carefully following on behind. The screech of an owl broke the silence of the night as they neared the edge of the first field of crops. The warriors all froze and stood waiting, listening for any sound their presence had been compromised. Jarl Bjorn spoke, "Come it's clear, let us move."

Meanwhile, Frode and his group had crossed over the sluice channel, using the irrigation gate from the river, he made the men jog down along the sluice channel's length to reach the track that ran the other side of the village. The small group stood, leaning on shields and spears to get their breath back. Healfden approached Frode, leaned in, and spoke with him "Frode why did we rush to get here, the men are having to catch their breath." Frode frowned " My young Lord we had twice the distance to cover than your Jarl father, we needed to be in position to see him at his point of attack, look there to the left of the buildings, then that way we can circle the settlements to launch our attack as a unit." "If I'd not pushed the men we would not arrive in time to support your father." "Don't worry when we attack the men's battle blood will rise and they will soon forget that they have just had a hard run carrying weapons."

"You'll learn my young Lord that our men are strong warriors they just need to be kept busy and not have time to think about what they are about to undertake thinking and strategy is your job with the help of able captains like me." Healfden looked into Frodes eyes and understood what he meant, Healfden looked at his three companions from childhood Arn, Bo, and Berg, he looked at all three then back to Frode. Healfden spoke "Frode, would you take Arn and tutor him so he can learn from you?" Frode looked hard at his young Lord "No I'll take Berg, I have seen him fight he is calm and in control, and readily helps a weaker warrior, he should be your chosen Captain when you take your father's position, I'd also send Bo to train with Orm at sailing Roar as Orm said he'd helped him during the last sailings up the river and can also speak different languages fluently he will best serve you as Steersman and captain of any fleet." Healfden nodded "Thank you Frode. I will think about what you say and speak with Father regards this."

Frode looked towards the fields hearing a distant owl screech "We shall move closer now nice and slow, stay alert men, don't be heard we need the attack to be a surprise."

The two groups of warriors slowly moved forward to the huddle of buildings. Jarl Bjorn went through the details in his mind again, they knew from earlier visits as traders that the families were housed in the three small thatched wooden cottages at the side of the larger cottage. The larger cottage was empty as its owner was on guard duty for the Thane, he would be standing across the river in the old watchtower looking towards Powy's. The small close-knit family and community this night should have no more than six men of various ages and four women with around a dozen children of all ages. They would all be easy pickings for his seasoned warriors.

Jarl Bjorn stood and watched as Frodes men split into groups to stand by the entrance to each small cottage, he sent two of his own to watch the barns and others to stand at the rear of the cottages in case anyone tried to escape. He looked around at his warriors then at

Frode he said one word "GO" and released his warriors to war on the peaceful community. Frode smashed his foot against the first small wooden door shattering it easily into splinters of wood, he ducked under the low lintel and stepped quickly into the cottage with another warrior close behind him. The screams started echoing around the still, peaceful night. Healfden and Berg attacked the second cottage Berg splintered the door with a swing of his axe. He shouted and ran inside, Orm ran his shoulder at the third cottage but stopped short as it opened. A man sword and axe in hand ran out heading straight at Orm. He was followed by a youth clutching a seax and axe in his small hands. Orm ducked as the man swung the sword narrowly missing his head, Orm rolled jumped, turned, and blocked a swing from the axe. Bo stepped forward thrusting his shield out above Orm's head to save him then back swung his axe to hack at the man's sword arm. The screams rent the air as the blood fountains over Orm and Bo from the missing hand. Stepping to his right Bo smashed his axe into the man's head ending his life.

Meanwhile, the youth was slowly pushed back to the entrance of the doorway by Orm's righthand man though only young he was fighting hard and even managed to steal a strike against Orm's man. Orm stood walked forward swung his axe down to wreck the youth's shoulder and drive down into his heart, a slow sigh escaped his lips as he dropped dead to the floor as the blood ran from his body to stain the hard-packed mud floor.

Frode had remerged from the cottage his blade thick with blood, a screaming bundle of a pale body in remnants of clothing dragged behind him by its hair. Frode was laughing loudly "That was too easy Bjorn but look at this little beauty I found." The evil grin on Jarl Bjorn's face was evident to the young girl he dragged her from Forde's grasp pulling her along, she screamed something deep inside told her that this was going to be very unpleasant.

Healfden and Berg both emerged with blood-red weapons, Healfden also dragged a female out by the ankle, more sport to be had her night clothes bundled up above her waist as she was dragged along the hard-packed yard her pale nakedness seen in the waning moonlight.

The warriors appeared from the rear of the cottages also dragging victims and throwing them to the floor in a heap of half-naked squirming flesh. Jarl Bjorn licked his lips in anticipation as he looked down at the huddle of young female flesh before him, the bloodletting and half-naked women adding to his growing arousal.

The warriors looked at the young women almost drooling in anticipation, hoping that their Jarl would allow them some pleasures of the flesh before they made their escape.

"Well done, that was easy, we will have some fun in a while, firstly see what provisions we can load into the cart and take away with us, then drag the rest of the bodies out into the open Frode deal with it Healfden, Orm you stay with me and we will watch these women" Frode nodded grabbing warriors and directing them to tasks, he spoke to one warrior "Eldritch, not you go up the track and keep watch for anyone coming from the village, we don't think anyone got away but let's be safe" Eldritch nodded throwing his shield over his shoulder and walked away. Frode walked around the area checking that the men were busy, the cart was piled high with food, ale, and trinkets.

WHILE HE AND the men were busy. Orm could hear the screams of horror and pain from some of the women as his Jarl and son beat and raped them talking about their pleasure however and with whomever, they wanted. Frode strode to the furthest barn and could see Berg checking a wooden crate he turned and looked at Frode, "Look at this wooden crate full of red wine, want some?" Frode smiled "Yes why not let us share a quick bottle, while our Jarl enjoys himself" Berg took the top off and took a long drink smiling he passed the bottle over "Pretty Good stuff, I'd rather have this than rape some unfortunate young girl" Frode drank deeply from the bottle handing it back " I agree very tasty, our Jarl always takes his pleasure, I have stopped advising him against it, you will learn that sometimes our advice is ignored" Berg smiled "Well then let us finish this bottle, there are five more what shall I do with them?" Frode grinned "Hide them we will have them later when back in camp" Berg nodded and Frode moved on to hurry the warriors along.

Jarl Bjorn and Healfden had beaten and raped the young women, they now all lay huddled in a group sobbing and wailing, beaten, and bruised physically and mentally. Healfden stood laughing as he finished his final insult and urinated over them. Jarl Bjorn looked around he could see some of his warriors moving the cart it was over halfway across the fields, and the bodies of the dead were all thrown out into the yard. He turned to Frode "Call Eldritch back in and fire the village then we can move off, by the time you get back across the fields we should be loaded and ready to sail"

Frode nodded " Yes Bjorn I will keep Berg and Eldritch we can fire the buildings between us while the rest of the men assist you."

"Good" responded Jarl Bjorn "I will move off then"

Frode watched Bjorn go and turned to both Berg and Eldritch " Come let us light some brands up, leave your shields and swords at the field edge and we will pick them up when we leave. We will start with the barns as they still have food in them and will take longer to light"

The three men stacked their equipment and started to light brands and then the barn and farm cottages. The raped girls lay in a group on the floor, still huddled together as Frode passed them to reach the fields he noticed fresh blood on them where someone had stabbed them through with a sword. "Such a waste," Berg said to Frode as he passed by. Frode nodded "Yes we could have taken those to the slave market they would have raised a pretty penny or two, let us away lads we have a ride to catch, time for a quick run."

The men slung shields and strapped weapons and set off at a steady pace along the well-used footpath back to the pier and Roar,

Berg glanced over his shoulder at the death and destruction they left behind. He sighed such was the way of the world the weak always suffered and the strong abused, raped, and killed them without care or compassion. The weak were seen as a commodity to be used by the strong.

CHAPTER 3
THE DEVASTATION

The sentry stood along the southern wall of the village and was the first to notice a flicker of light away at Crag Rock. He stood a few moments watching and looking he was unsure what was happening.

He turned and shouted to his fellow further along the village wall. "Hey, look over at Crag Rock, what do you think is happening?"

The two sentries both stood staring out into the night sky. Orange and red flashes lit the buildings of Crag Rock up. Then dark black smoke started to bellow upwards as the flames danced over the buildings. "Quick sound the alarm" The first sentry shouted to his comrade

The man looked once more over the wall and could see the flames clearly now. He ran to the horn hung on a rope by the gate and blew loud and hard into it to wake the village.

Other sentries down by the second gate and further round the wall ran to see what the issue was. A senior warrior appeared Thornhed a junior to Captain Lavos, "What's going on here" He shouted loudly pushing the other men out of the way as he walked the length of the wall to stand in the small gate tower.

THE BETRAYAL

"It's Crag Rock; look I think it's been attacked" answered the first man.

Thornhed looked across and could see the flames and smoke engulfing the homes and barns of the small settlement. He sighed and turned "You" pointing at a sentry " Go and make sure Captain Lavos is awake, advise him of the issue, then ask if he wishes me to take any men out to Crag Rock." He turned from the sentry who set off with a leap down from the platform around the village wall towards the captain's quarters next to the Thane's Hall, the sentry was not looking forward to waking the grim Captain Lavos.

Thornhed stood watching looking over the area of the walled village and the old Roman bridge and wooden pier next to the river, he looked across the river to the small broken-down watchtower which more of the Thane's men stood guard at, a thin cruel smile was on Thornhed's face as he watched the silhouettes of the men on guard Raulf, Trevik, and Alun.

Time ticked on as Thornhed watched the flames and smoke grow around Crag Rock he sent the sentries back to their posts and told them to stay alert, while he watched the river and flames waiting for his captain to attend the wall.

Lavos appeared in the dark next to Thornhed looking over the wall and the burning Crag Rock. He too slowly smiled and glanced towards the watchtower over the river, he looked at Thornhed "Any sign of the enemy?" Thornhed turned and shook his head "No all quiet here, looks like Crag Rock has been attacked and plundered."

The ladder behind them creaked as Thane Eldrig and his daughter Eleen appeared on the platform to look over the wall.

"Captain" Eleen boldly spoke, "What's the problem?"

Lavos slowly turned to look at Eleen who felt a shiver of fear down her spine as he looked hard into her eyes.

"It looks like raiders have attacked Crag Rock my Lady; it is in flames. I fear that they will all be dead or captured, and the winter stores stolen or destroyed." Lavos tried to look sad but utterly failed, Eleen knew that Lavos was a cruel hard man and hated the residents of Crag Rock as they were all old staunch supporters of her father's family.

Thane Eldrig spoke, "Lavos this is not good, send men to the watchtower to relieve Raulf and his men, then have them and you meet me in my hall, we need to discuss this urgently."

Lavos sneered his reply "Yes, Thane" and walked off into the night.

"Father" whispered Eleen "I don't trust him" she spoke quietly watching Lavos as he walked into the dark he soon disappeared from her sight as if the very darkness had consumed him.

"Hush child" was Eldrig's only response to her, he stood hands gripping the wall watching the flames and smoke rise high into the sky.

These past months had been most troublesome. The raiders had become much bolder since this new Jarl had arrived, Eldrig had lost men, horses, supplies, and shelters, and now this direct raid on the settlement of Crag Rock he knew in his heart that when he met with Raulf it was going to be a difficult conversation with him, and he would demand instant action from him.

Eleen his only remaining child stood beside him and gripped his hand. He felt the warmth and love from it he sighed so like her mother. What would become of her after he was gone, he needed to ensure her safety, Eleen must be married and soon.

Eleen stood watching and looked towards the river, she looked hard and gasped "Father, look a boat on the bend further past Crag Rock"

Her father and Thornhed turned and looked to where Eleen was pointing. Eldrig sighed heavily well we know who is responsible now child, come let us be away to the hall if you could get some drinks ready for when Lavos returns with Raulf, I feel this will not go well with him tonight, Crag Rock is the family home and has been for decades.

THE BETRAYAL

Slowly Eldrig and Eleen walked across the open area of the village back to the main hall where Eleen was soon busy rushing around with the servants to prepare drinks and food for the men. Eleen knew Raulf well he had served her father and her father's father before him and was a strong dependable warrior, proud and protective of his friends and family her father was right it would be a difficult conversation, Raulf would be stricken with grief.

Lavos had left Eldrig and Eleen on the wall as he walked across the darkened village to the far wall and the small gate that stood facing the river. This gate was only used by the warriors as access to the river and the sentry tower across the bridge of the river. When looking up from the river across the rock cliff face it seemed that there was no passageway through to the walled village, but one small steep path was hidden in the crevices and a single file of men could carefully walk the path.

As Lavos walked the village he saw the twins Hardison and Loff the village hunters appear from their small cabin. He would send them to relieve Raulf at the watchtower.

Hardison, Loff do you have your weapons to hand Lavos asked.

"Yes" was the sharp reply from Hardison.

"Good, through the gate with both of you and take over duty at the watchtower then send Raulf, Alun, and Trevik back here and tell them to report to me in the Thane's Hall, and that the Thane is waiting on them." The twins looked at Lavos who snarled at them "NOW, move it, Go, you blundering idiots."

With that, he turned from them and walked back across the village.

The two brothers looked at each other shrugged their shoulders and headed towards the small, guarded gate. Thrun was on duty at the gate and saw the twins appear " What is going on lads" he enquired" The twins were not known for their conversations. They quickly looked at each other before Hardison replied, "Do not know really, we are going to the watchtower to stand duty." and with that, he helped Thrun, and Loff lift the two heavy oak bars that locked the gate.

THRUN STOOD in the gateway as he watched the two nimble brothers sprint down the rocky path jumping and weaving through the crevices, he decided he would stand and wait with the gate open for the return of the other men, well he sure was not going to get those oak bars back in place alone they were much too heavy. Thrun could smell the smoke and knew trouble lay ahead.

AT THE WATCHTOWER, Alun had seen the first flickers of flames across at Crag Rock. He had groaned when he realized what this could mean and turned to his old friend Raulf to inform him, "Raulf, look Crag Rock it is aflame" By the time Raulf had climbed up the ladders to the watchtower the flames were high in the sky lighting up the night sky. Raulf was quiet, he stood watching his face grim against the small glow from the torch above Alun's head. Alun looked at his friend knowing the sadness Raulf would be feeling, he noticed Raulf gripping the rail around the watchtower his fingers wrapped tightly around the rail turning white as he gripped harder and harder. Trevik was standing in the doorway at the bottom of the watchtower he noticed the light as the gateway had opened then as he continued to watch he saw two shapes running across the old Roman bridge. He shouted up to the others " Looks like we have company I would say it is the twins from how they are running"

Alun replied, " Good we will come down and see what is wrong" was he his reply he turned to Raulf " Come my old friend let's climb down, this must be urgent for the Thane to send them across."

. . .

THE BETRAYAL

Alun and Trevik crossed the bridge after the grim-faced Raulf, they both knew trouble lay ahead for the trio. Raulf for the first time as a warrior of the Thane disobeyed the order to attend his hall. Crossing the old Roman bridge, the three friends circled the rock face where the village and hall stood cutting across the woods, he reached the edge of the fields that he owned and managed with his family. The closer Raulf got to Crag Rock the quicker he went. Alun and Trevik both ambled on behind he did not turn to check he knew these men would follow him if he asked it or not, such was the warrior brotherhood they had.

Raulf could smell the burning, panic, anger, and frustration muddled his sensors. Raulf could hear someone saying his name but stomped on one heavy foot after the other. A huge hand grabbed him Raulf swung round grim vacant look on his face but with a seax in his hand, he stopped tears glazing his eyes. "Raulf" spoke Trevik quietly "We need to take care, there could still be attackers around."

Raulf stopped his shoulders sagging he knew deep in his heart he was too late. "Yes, my friend I am sorry you are right, I will head in here, you circle right, and you Alun left go careful and quiet. The three looked at each other over clasped arms and strode confidently as only seasoned warriors do into Crag Rock. The bodies of all his family were here it seemed not a soul had survived. Raulf had not a single family member alive to continue his line and manage Crag Rock he didn't even know if his cousin still lived who served Lord Ludeca.

Alun spoke "Raulf, come quickly" Raulf turned to see Alun kneeling over a small bundle of rags, his heart stopped Sareen, no Sareen his smiling always happy young niece. Raulf bounded over dropping to his knees and hugging Sareen close " Oh my poor child he sobbed"

Sareen's small face looked up at her uncle a small curl of her lip and her eyes flickered she was near to death but felt so safe now her uncle held her close, her body shook from the pain and shock of this evil dark night. Raulf stroked Sareen's blood-splattered hair she had been roughly treated and abused before being stabbed by a sword her lifeblood was leaking over the dry-packed earth. Sareen opened her mouth and gulped in the air two names came rushing from her mouth Bjorn, and Healfden as she sobbed and tried to tell of the attack. Then as the air expelled from her tiny frame her soul departed. Raulf sobbed holding her to him then a huge rage of a roar escaped his mouth. Raulf sounded like a mythical beast as he roared out his anger and frustration. They wasted lives for no apparent reason. He sat rocking with Sareen in his arms tears dropped off his old, rugged face to drop onto her cheek.

THE THREE FRIENDS dug graves at what would have been the entrance to Crag Rock. The bodies were wrapped in any cloth or blankets that could be found. The direct families are placed together. The three men buried all of Raulf's family and placed small wooden markers on the graves before trudging shocked and slowly back to the village to finally report to Thane Eldrig some hours later than expected.

LAVOS MET them at the gate shouting abuse at the men for the state they had appeared in covered in soil, ash, blood, and stinking like animals. The man's hand went to their weapons, and they would have used them if not for Eleen appearing walking across the open village area towards them.

"Raulf "she cried out "Come, please tell me of tonight, how your kin are." The blank look she received from the three warriors told her everything without a word passing their lips, gripped with grief and terror Eleen fell to her knees, face in her hands sobbing uncontrollably.

Raulf bent on one knee lifting Eleens's face tenderly with his grimy hands "Come child we must speak with your father."

At this point, Raulf had calmed. He needed to remain so when speaking with his Thane. But he knew deep inside that he would anger quickly and would end up arguing with his Thane. This dark night was proving difficult and would continue to be.

THANE ELDRIG SAT on the raised platform behind the top table, Lavos stood to one side and Eleen walked round to seat herself beside her father. Eleen turned to speak with her father who held up his hand to discourage her. Eldrig remained seated and spoke " Raulf, I should chide you for the lateness of my summons." Thane Eldrig sighed "Though I do understand the reason, my old friend. Come tell us what has happened."

Raulf did not answer at first his face a grim mask behind the mud, ash, blood, and tears.

He composed himself, standing tall, and looked up and spoke firmly "Thane Eldrig, my whole kin of Crag Rock are slaughtered, the women raped and killed, Crag Rock is no more the stores are destroyed, the eel traps shattered flooding the crops and fields. I no longer have the kin or the will to rebuild Crag Rock the seat of Crag Rock gifted to my forefathers by your forefathers. I return to you with a heavy heart and ask if I and my friends can be released from your service to track these Raiders down, the scum who have slaughtered my kin and loved ones. I need revenge, Thane, it is simmering like a hot boiling cauldron deep inside me."

THANE ELDRIG SLUMPED in his chair he had expected anger, frustration, and harsh words this composed speech by Raulf had unnerved him. It was Lavos who exploded with rants and harsh words in response.

Lavos leaned on the table slamming his fist hard down onto the table tipping plates and cups from it as he shouted spittle flew from his mouth. As he shouted abuse at the three old warriors.

Thane Eldrig stood, looking at his Captain, speaking calmly "Lavos SIT and be STILL" Lavos turned to his Thane anger in his eyes, how he wanted to spill the guts of this weak old man but now was not the time, no not now later he sighed and turned, and stepped away, his anger slowly subsiding he sat down on a bench watching and waiting to see what would now be decided.

Thane Eldrig looked to his daughter Eleen then to Raulf and then to his two loyal friends Trevik and Alun. He knew if he denied these men the justice that was so truly theirs to have, then one morning he would find the three men gone along with horses, weapons, and food. Thane Eldrig sighed he could ill afford to lose these men they were loyal and steadfast, safe hands to help the younger scared warriors, but he could not deny them the chance of retribution and he would not do so.

Eleen shook her father from his thoughts " Father, your decision?" was her question.

Eldrig looked at Eleen seeing her worried, concerned face and sighed he sat down composed himself, and took a drink. "Raulf, Trevik, and Alun come sit at my table as my friends one more time and drink with me we will discuss the merits of your plan. I presume you have a plan, my old friends?"

Raulf shrugged he had not a plan in mind, but knew he now needed one. Raulf thought quickly he now knew his Thane was willing to consent to them leaving and he also realised then that Eldrig would

THE BETRAYAL

wish for other men to accompany him. Raulf glanced quickly at Lavos, he had never trusted this, captain. It was strange Lavos had never crossed Raulf, but Raulf knew he wished to be more than he was and that was why Raulf had stayed close to his Thane these last years.

SLAVES BROUGHT MORE benches and fresh food as Raulf, Trevik, and Alun seated themselves Lavos moved and also sat down, he wanted to learn what was to happen if the plan went his way, then these three warriors would soon be absent, and hopefully disposed of.

THANE ELDRIG and the others sat talking and planning, he would ultimately decide on the final plan. Lavos and a group of his warriors along with Raulf, Trevik, and Alun would track the Raiders. If the opportunity to teach them a lesson came then if the risk was not great, they would seek justice. If and this was important the risk was too great Lavos, and his men could return, and if Raulf and his two loyal friends wished to stay and risk all on revenge then they were free to do so released from the Thane's duties they were now free men if they survived and returned to the village Eldrig agreed to support them as loyal sworn men once more.

Lavos sat listening to Raulf as he spoke with Eldrig, he was getting more annoyed as they spoke once he knew he was going to be also sent out. Lavos was fuming inside but tried to remain composed as he listened and agreed to track the raiders, he now needed to put a plan in place himself, Raulf and his friends could not be allowed to return to the village, their lives must be ended he could not have them return to continue in their support of Eldrig. But how would he manage this, Wigson, he needed Wigson to journey to Jarl Bjorn. Lavos had no other option. But how would he manage it, and would the Jarl even accommodate Wigson and listen to the plan? Well, he was prepared to risk Wigson's life on the venture.

CHAPTER 4
THE PLAN

Lavos was not happy when the meeting had ended, he stormed across the open yard to search out some of his loyal men. This had not been what he had planned not at all. He had hoped that Eldrig would allow Raulf and his bum-licking friends to just leave, leave and race after the Raiders and die in a glorious fight to the death that would leave him free to make his move, get rid of Eldrig and take over, but no he was expected to go hunt the raiders, Lavos was fuming as he stepped out across the yard, a dog scampered in front of him Lavos kicked the poor animal which whimpered as he angrily stomped to the small wooden wall.

Lavos stomped hard up the ladders of the wall he slammed his foot down so hard he broke a slat of the ladder and nearly tumbled off this did not improve his temper when he reached the wall's top.

The night air was chilly as Lavos stood looking over the village wall he breathed slow and deep to calm himself and concentrate on the

THE BETRAYAL

task at hand. What was he to do now, he must adapt the plan but how. As he stood looking out towards Crag Rock, he felt the thud of feet approaching him along the timber walkway around the wall.

"Lavos" he turned to see Wigson walking the platform on his turn of duty this night. "What irks you tonight, not getting laid by a slave girl, he laughed"

Wigson, though a close friend and ally of Lavos had just unwittingly overstepped the boundary. Quick as the snake that Lavos was his arm snapped out firmly gripping Wigson by the throat. His maul of a fist tightened around his neck almost crushing the windpipe. Wigson struggled to breathe flapping his arms around to stop Lavos. Panic in his eyes as he tried to escape the grip of death, Wigson was struggling to breathe and feeling faint.

"Arsehole" muttered Lavos as he dropped Wigson spluttering and gasping for air as he sucked in deeply to fill his lungs with much needed air, his body sucked in the cold night air desperately.

Eventually, on his knees, Wigson looked up at Lavos who once more stood looking over the wall. " What the, why," he spluttered at Lavos. As he gasped for urgently needed breath.

"The plans changed Eldrig the whimpering fool wants me and some of you to accompany the idiots as they seek revenge." He said as he stared into the dark night once more lost in his thoughts of how to overcome the problem.

Wigson didn't speak he knew now was not the right time to remind Lavos that Wigson had voiced these very concerns when he and the others had discussed the plans, Wigson had said all along that Eldrig would send men out after the raiders and it was foolish to think overwise, that comment had cost him a meaty punch to his stomach leaving him feeling sick and a dark purple bruise for days as a reminder not to speak out against Lavos.

W<small>IGSON WAS NOT</small> a great fighter but was a good thinker and planner and these attributes had led him to his current position supporting the captain he had acted as a go between on plenty of underhand deals that had reaped rewards of money for himself and Lavos, Wigson shrewd as always had made sure he benefitted more than Lavos, but that was his fault if he trusted Wigson so much. What to advise Lavos now would be the next problem to ponder. He decided to stay quiet and see what Lavos came up with first Lavos was already enraged it would be better if he let Lavos plan before he spoke up.

L<small>AVOS LOOKED</small> at Wigson still sitting on the floor smiling down on him Lavos knew what he wanted, " I have a job for you my friend you will not like it but if you do not do it, I will speak with Raulf and ensure he believes you responsible for these treacherous acts this very night, so we don't have to go out hunting and then think of another way to dispatch him.." That cruel smile slowly returned to Lavos's face; he knew he had won the discussion.

Wigson still sat slowly using the wall and pulled himself upright to look Lavos in the eye. " You would not" he asked. The hard stare he received back told him Lavos would. Wigson was trapped he would have no choice but to obey Lavos dam the man thought Wigson Lavos had me by the balls this time.

L<small>AVOS LOOKED</small> hard at Wigson and explained he was to leave as soon as possible and alone, and before he and the rest of the party would be ready to set off. Lavos would say he had sent Wigson to scout the area in front to try and find the route the raiders had travelled and

THE BETRAYAL

mark the route for the others to follow. Wigson was to ensure that the group travelled a certain route that Lavos had already planned in his head, the idea was to have the group travel through unpopulated areas further inland and then circle back towards the river where it ran through a valley and a large, wooded area. Wigson knew this area well and could travel fast over it to mark the route to follow.

LAVOS SUPPLIED a message for Wigson as he needed him to locate the raiders inform them of the change to the plan and assist with finalising a solution to be rid of Raulf and his friends at last.

LAVOS HELD Wigson by his shoulder as he spoke: " Listen, my friend, it is imperative you find the bloody raider scum and inform them I need them to be in the woods at the bottom of Lythe Valley three days from now, we will camp in the small clearing on the east side of the woods, I will make sure that Raulf is on guard duty with his little friends and then the scum can sort the problem for us." Lavos looked around him quickly making sure nobody else had heard, but only he and Wigson stood on the wall. Lavos spoke again he knew he needed Wigson now more than ever to be his lapdog "Wigson more than anyone here you are the one I trust; you are aware we need rid of Raulf and companions to make our move" Wigson nodded looking back into Lavos hard eyes " I know Lavos, but this is desperate the raiders could kill me just out of spite" replied Wigson. Lavos nodded " I won't lie you are correct but think of the rewards when we succeed, and succeed we will, you know plenty of ways to make money we can make huge profits in slaves and you will manage this I am aware you are shrewd and have exploited people, including me of money, you will be my right-hand man when I have the village" Lavos paused smiling at Wigson "Are you with me, my friend?"

Wigson slowly nodded "Aye Lavos, I am with you till the end as always, let us hope this is all worth it."

. . .

Lavos and Wigson climbed down the ladders and walked across the courtyard towards the stables. Wigson turned leaving Lavos, and hurried to his quarters he required his spear, bow, and arrows to go with his seax, war axe, and shield. Lavos headed inside the stable to ready a horse, he grabbed a stableman asleep in the hay "You go to the kitchen grab some bread, cheese dried meat, and a bag of oats, and be quick about it, oh and a skin of ale tell the staff that I Lavos have sent you" the young man set off at pace across the yard he knew he might be able to grab some extra food for himself and his stable friends if he was quick while the cook bagged the items that captain Lavos required, he smiled and ran faster.

Meanwhile, Lavos chose a solid looking chestnut mare for Wigson to ride he put some food out for the horse to eat while he quickly brushed the horse down checking its legs and hoofs before throwing a blanket and saddle over its back, he rolled a second blanket up tied it securely to the rear of the saddle and hung a net of hay too, the extra blanket would keep Wigson warm at night and the hay would keep the horse fed. Lavos led the horse out of the stable into the open yard he could see the outline of Wigson approaching with his bow, arrows, and shield slung over his back, his seax and war axe hung from his belt and a spear in his gloved hands, as Wigson neared Lavos could see he had his battered helmet on and leather padded jacket. Lavos smiled and nodded " You look ready" Wigson just nodded and then swung onto the horse.

The young stable man was running back across the yard panting "Captain, here are the supplies you wished for, cook added a few apples too, and a piece of dried fish" smiling at Lavos and hoping he had done well. Lavos took the bag and hung it upon the saddle, " And what did you manage to steal while in the kitchen he asked" the stable man gulped in fear Lavos laughed " Keep whatever you stole as a reward but share it with your friends, now run and tell the men to open the gate for me, quickly now."

"Thank you" he quickly replied and ran across the yard to the darkness of the gate.

Lavos looked at Wigson "You know what to do and where to go and what must happen."

Wigson looked at Lavos and replied "Yes"

With that Lavos turned holding the reins he led the mare and Wigson across the yard towards the gate which was even now slowly being pulled open. The gateway was lit now as two guards pulled the gate open and the stable man held a torch flickering in the wind casting shadows across the gate and the village wall.

Lavos led Wigson out through the gate to the track outside he waved the guards to stand by the gate and wait and walked a short distance away so as not to be heard.

"Wigson, ride fast but carefully, head out to Crag Rock and ride around the village a few times then across the fields to the old jetty, from there travel down the river and follow its path before heading West you should find their tracks easily enough to follow from the river as they head to the pass above Lythe Valley. The Jarl's holding is on the west valley I would advise you to follow the direct path that they would have taken from the river across the old Roman road and past the old fort, then skirt the wood and head up the old track over Lythe Valley and circle to the west to reach the holding they have on the hill, you should be in consent view of them from the moment you skirt the wood so I would advise you be extra careful from this point ride slowly and carefully and keep your hands away from your weapons."

Wigson sat and listened to Lavos and took note of the journey he needed to make he should reach the woods by this time tomorrow if all went to plan. He looked at Lavos "Let's hope I see you in the woods before" he replied

Lavos nodded " Yes, you need to be back to meet us I would prefer it if you could reach us somewhere near the old Roman road, you need to leave markers on the route to prove you have passed that way"

Wigson smiled "OK I will use the crescent moon shape as a marker for you to follow" he looked at Lavos "Let us hope those Cretans do not kill me before I can get the plan in place and don't expect me to go up the sword on the sword with Raulf, I am good but even at his older age he is still faster than me."

Lavos nodded " I agree we need to let the Raider scum deal with them, we cannot afford any mistakes, travel well my friend succeed in this, and we will prevail"

Wigson kicked his heel into the horse and set off at a slow trot down the hard-packed dirt track from the settlement towards the main road. Which then led towards Crag Rock before then turning further inland to the richer countryside and larger settlements of the kingdom of Mercia ruled by King Offa.

WIGSON LOOKED around him as he trotted the road towards Crag Rock, the air had a chill or was it just the situation he was now in, he slowed the horse as he reached Crag Rock the stench of death was overwhelming, as he reached the centre of the settlement, he could see the blood all over the hard-packed floor. He'd heard from others that the women had been brutally raped by the raiders before they had been murdered. Wigson was used to death and wanton killing as a warrior, but the rape of women and especially young girls was a step too far for him, but he knew that was why the attack had been planned so. It had been Jarl Bjorn and Lavo's intention to submit the settlement to wanton, brutal, rape, and killings. Lavos had said it needed a deep depth of pain to send a shockwave to Thane Eldrig to make sure he would take desperate action and mistakes, and also Lavos wanted to hit Raulf hard.

Wigson though did not understand the hatred that Lavos had for Raulf, he understood Raulf would stand with Thane Eldrig and his family, but Wigson had suggested a silent killing with no fuss, a quick blade one dark night on the way back from sentry duty a quick sneak attack by some hired men, Wigson was aware of small bands of rogues who would have undertaken the killings for a few coins, but no Lavos wanted it more dramatic than that... idiot.

So now Wigson had to implement the new plan. Great he thought in the shit once more.

Wigson rode on cutting through the fields and towards the river he just wanted to make sure that all the Jarls men had left before he cut down and followed the river, he had an idea where the raiders would have landed, a few miles downriver. He could then follow the old trading trail, which met the Roman road further inland. Wigson was not unduly worried about this part of the trip it would be when he reached the Old Fort and headed out to Lythe Valley, he would be vulnerable at this point. Wigson pondered as he rode, he had a difficult task ahead of him once he reached the Jarl and his men, they were not known for listening and taking advice. He knew he would have to be very careful with his words to the Jarl and his son Healfden. He was definitely a hot head, Wigson remembered the first time he and Lavos had met them when they had gone to King Offa's capital on behalf of Thane Eldrig, the mad glint in Healfden's eyes as he spoke of slaughter, rape, and murder. He was like a man possessed, very dangerous, and would easily just slit your throat just for the hell of it.

CHAPTER 5
THE TRIP

The air had a chill to it but then it was always cooler nearer to the river, Wigson looked up into the night sky, hardly any cloud showed, and the stars shone brightly. He kept the horse to a slow walk even though he could easily see he was not about to let the horse run when any tuft of grass could potentially hide a rabbit hole to trip and injure the horse and possibly, himself. Wigson rode on humming a tune, he wanted to make some distance before he stopped for a few hour's rest.

THE HORSE SNORTED and Wigson suddenly alert, something was out there, he slowed the horse and stopped looking towards the long grass to his left he quietly pulled his bow out quickly notching an arrow in preparation, the grass rustled once more the long strands of grass parted to reveal the head of a young deer it looked straight at him its eyes wide with panic jumped from the grass and set to run away from him and the river Wigson released the arrow which took the young deer straight through the neck blood splattered the long grass and the shoulder of the deer it jumped just once to run then collapsed to the floor it's life slowly ebbing from it, blood pumping over the grass.

He climbed from the horse hooking the bow across his saddle horn, grabbing his knife he bent slicing the neck as the deer gave one last shudder, He removed and cleaned the arrow it was good to be used again. Then swiftly gutted the deer before throwing it over the horse. Once more in the saddle, he continued, Wigson knew that when he turned onto the trading trail a short distance on where two old oak trees one still standing tall and proud the other lay twisted, charred, and broken from a storm some years back but the location would be great for him to rest and roast the deer, he could safely tie the horse up and have the tree at his back for shelter and the charred tree as a barrier for protection.

Wigson soon reached the trees, he secured the horse laid out his blanket, and collected twigs and branches to get a small fire going. He skillfully skinned the deer with his small sharp knife, he liked the knife it was a great tool especially when used for quiet killings slicing it across the throat of an unsuspecting victim. He quickly cut the carcass into four chunks two he placed on a branch to roast over the open fire, the other two he wrapped in dandelion and nettles and placed them into the hot embers of the fire then put more branches on to keep the heat in. The two in the embers would cook slowly overnight to eat the following day. He wrapped himself in his blanket after feeding the horse he had some bread and cheese to eat while he waited for the deer to cook through. He sat in silence listening. He knew the raiders were nearby he had spotted them a while ago as he approached the trees to make camp, that was why he had cooked the deer the smell would hopefully encourage them to investigate who he was and why he was here, he hoped with the food on offer the men would show themselves and he would have the chance to talk with them and hoped to be escorted to the Jarl's Hall.

What had surprised Wigson the most was how early he was on the trail to have contacted the Jarl's men, Wigson had not reached the Old Roman Fort at the approach to Lythe Valley. The three men had seen the stranger approach from the river, they slowly shadowed him keeping to the trees to watch his direction of travel. Once he stopped and they realized he was making camp, they also tied their horses up and slowly crept close to observe him, they noticed straight away he was a warrior seeing he wore chainmail a shield and sat propped against the burnt tree trunk with a bow and quiver of arrows next to it, they saw the war axe laid next to the blanket and when he walked to the fire to check the roasting meet the sword and seax strapped around his waist. This was an able and experienced warrior, and they would not find it easy to kill him, it could if they were not careful mean the death of one of them. The three men all experienced fighters of Jarl Bjorn welcomed a fight and understood it could end their life but would not die for nothing. They sat watching as the warrior slowly turned the roasting meat the fat dripping and sizzling on the fire, the smell of the meat was delicious as it wafted through the trees towards them, and their stomachs growled in anticipation of the tender juicy meat.

Wigson smiled to himself as he turned the meat once more, he knew the men were in the trees to his left. He believed there were three of them but no more than four, the smell of the roasting deer would be making them hungry by now. He stood and stepped towards the large burnt tree taking out his seax he quickly stripped away a large section of bark breaking it into four to use as plates for the meat. He placed the bark on the grass beside the fire and slowly carved a piece from the haunch of the deer he quickly devoured the tasty morsel nosily licking his fingers clean. He laughed deep and loud "Will you not join me, my friends, I am aware you are watching in the trees" silence greeted him. Wigson spoke again "My friends I have freshly roasted deer, bread, and cheese if you wish to share my food come sit by the fire" The trees rustled to his left and three warriors stepped towards him. shields across their back and swords in their scabbards so visible threat. "Come," said Wigson turning and kneeling by the fire he quickly carved strips of meat off the first haunch of deer dropping it onto the strips of bark, he walked to his pack next to the shield pulling the bread and cheese out and sliced this into chunks to add to the meat sat on the bark.

Whilst he had done this the three warriors had approached and stood across the fire from him.

"Sit my friends, sit and eat," said Wigson to them, the three warriors looked at each other, the middle of the three nodded his head and the three sat down, Wigson now knew who the leader was and who he needed to talk with to get his escort to Jarl Bjorn.

Wigson passed the men the tasty hot meat, bread, and cheese and began eating himself watching the three men who greedily wolfed the meat down wiping their greasy fingers on their animal-skinned cloaks. The middle warrior looked up and spoke "I am Tove this pointing to his right is Rune and this to his left is Svend and who are you?" Wigson smiled "Pleased to meet you Tove, Rune, and Svend I am named Wigson, I come to seek an audience with Jarl Bjorn I have a message from Captain Lavos for him." Wigson decided to get straight to the point he only hoped that these warriors knew of Lavos, and he would get passage.

TOVE STAYED silent while Wigson spoke eating the last of his bread and cheese, He looked at Wigson and then at the still-cooking meat " Is there more?" Wigson smiled thinking to himself I am glad I cooked some meat in the embers that I can eat later. "Of course, my new friend Tove, let me carve more for you all" Wigson replenished the men with more hot meat. Sitting once more opposite them and patiently waiting for a response.

Rune muttered something to Tove who nodded, and Svend shrugged his shoulders in response. Tove turned back to Wigson "Do you have any ale new friend Wigson" Wigson stood walking back to his pack pulling the skin of ale from it and passing it over the three smiled and then after taking a huge gulp of ale Tove spoke once more " We are men loyal to Jarl Bjorn, you are lucky Rune's younger brother Berg is a good warrior and a friend of the Jarls son Healfden he ventured out two nights ago so we are aware of who your captain is, though we do not understand why you have come we will take you through the pass to Jarl Bjorn's Hall, you can see if he will speak to you or just cut off your head we can promise nothing"

Wigson smiled back "My thanks Tove, Rune, Svend that would be most kind of you, please finish the ale I intend to sleep a while before we venture on"

Tove returned the smile "Our thanks, we will stay here by your fire, Svend will fetch our horses and we will set off before the sun rises so we may reach Jarl Bjorn's Hall after midday tomorrow"

Wigson nodded and went to his blanket keeping the axe and shield close by. Svend stood and walked back to the trees to return moments later with the horses. The three men striped the meat of the bones making sure none was left and ensured the Ale skin was empty too.

Wigson sat watching them he smiled it was okay, let them fill their bellies and drink their fill at least if anything happened, they would hopefully be slower than he, and victory should be his, but he hoped they would safely take him to Bjorn that was the next problem.

Wigson was up before the others packed up and ready to go, he pulled the leaf-wrapped meat from the embers stripping it from the bones, then wrapped it in the linen from the bread, and stored it in his pack, he would not go hungry on the journey.

• • •

WIGSON WALKED to the bushes to relieve himself, Tove was awake now and kicking the others to rouse them, Tove did not look impressed when he saw Wigson standing by his horse ready to go while they were all asleep. The four of them were soon on their way, Rune was in front with Tove and Svend riding slightly to the rear of Wigson. Wigson smiled at the distrust of these men he had checked their horses while they slept and he knew if he ran his horse, they would not catch him, always have the advantage he thought to himself.

By the time, the sun was up they had reached the Old Roman Fort, Wigson looked at the hill of the fort with its deep ditch and imposing wall and tower even though it was now half ruined it would have been hard to attack and costly in lives, no wonder the Romans had conquered so much of the island. The group continued up the pathways skirting the wood and heading up Lythe Valley. The three men of Jarl Bjorn did not really talk with Wigson as they travelled the Valley to reach the Raider's settlement and ultimately Bjorn's Hall. Wigson noted the paths were well-travelled plenty of horses coming and going as well as the boot prints of men. The Jarl must have a reasonable number of men, if so, why did he want to support Lavos, surely, he did not need to. Something for Wigson to ponder on while he waited to meet with the Jarl. The trip passed quickly and soon Wigson could make out the palisade fence of the settlement, it stood at least the height of two men with a large wooden gate with two towers it was obvious that a walkway went around the full length of the wall too. A bastard to crack he said to himself.

CHAPTER 6
THE MEETING

Wigson walked his horse under the large double gate. He was impressed by the strength and size of the gate and the size of the two square towers above it which could easily hold around six men each. The gate was strong and double lengths of wood sat vertically and horizontally to each other therefore very strong to break down. A second gate stood at the inner end of the towers and fighting platforms again these were double strength. The palisade walls had a fighting platform and stocks of spears and shields at points all around it within easy reach of the raiders to defend the wall. Rune turned to Tove and spoke with him before looking at Wigson and riding off through the settlement towards the Jarls Hall. Wigson saw Svend and Tove start to climb from their horses and followed suit.

"Come," said Tove gesturing to follow them towards the stables. A few young lads came from within taking the horses from Svend and Tove an older youth approached Tove pointing at Wigson and his horse asking questions, Wigson could see Tove answering and pointing at the horse and pushing the gangly youth forward. The youth with a mop of matted ginger hair spoke, "If I could take your horse" he looked up at Wigson. "Of course, but please treat her good she is loyal and worked hard getting me here," replied Wigson. Handing the reins to the youth he turned to look at Tove, who just stood waiting.

Wigson was beginning to feel slightly uncomfortable as he stood in the open area the people of the settlement were watching him and he could feel some of the warriors around the palisade wall looking down at him. Wigson knew he was been left to wait on purpose, but it still left him on edge, he kept a calm composure it did not do to let the scum know how you actually felt.

WIGSON LOOKED AROUND and saw a small bench outside a building next to the stables an old woman sat repairing clothes her head down busy with her work, and a small, thatched canopy shielded her from the sun. Wigson slowly turned and walked over to the old woman and looked up, Wigson inclined his head and spoke to her "May I sit with you in the shade, while I await an invitation from the Jarl, if you have water or ale I would happily pay" The old women nodded her head at the empty seat beside her" Wigson smiled and sat down shrugging his cloak from his shoulders he looked across to Tove and Svend smiling at them both. The old women shouted in Danish through a small, shuttered window and a waif of a girl of around ten summers came running out with a skin of ale and some bread and cheese. Wigson turned to the old woman with his hand outstretched upon the open palm where coins of different value. The old woman eyed them eagerly, she would not dare to take too many as she would not wish to be accused of stealing, she looked at the coins and picked two of the smaller ones nodding her head in thanks. Wigson smiled and gave her a third coin.

TOVE AND SVEND looked annoyed they had stayed stood in the open with the sun blazing down, Wigson was smiling he had won a small victory as now when the messenger came from Jarl Bjorn, he would have to come to him as he sat relaxing eating and drinking. Time ticked by and Tove along with Svend still stood waiting, Wigson heard the sound of horses approaching from deep within the settlement, he stayed sat and closed his eyes pretending to be asleep.

"Excuse me," said a voice Wigson looked up he could see a young warrior with an expensive coat of mail and cloak he looked familiar it was then that Wigson thought this must be Berg the younger brother to Rune. Wigson stood and looked around he could see Rune had returned along with Berg and two other warriors. "Hello" smiled Wigson. "Jarl Bjorn will speak with you now if you would be so good as to follow me" Berg turned and stepped away taking a few steps before looking back to ensure Wigson was following. Berg took the reins of his horse from his brother and set off walking deeper into the settlement, Wigson stepped quickly to catch him and walk alongside him. "Nice day for a stroll" laughed Wigson Berg smiled " My Jarl would not wish you to go galloping around and get lost, you could, well anything could happen to you!" smiled Berg.

Wigson replied " True very true lead the way young man, lead the way"

Wigson was sure he was being taken on a circular route to the Hall, he was sure that he had passed a few of the crude buildings a few times even though they all looked very alike it was things like a stool outside a home and a bench where men sat drinking. Wigson was aware this was so he would not know the layout of the settlement. He was not interested they did not have enough men to attack the Jarl he had nearly double the men, many a lot fitter and younger, and all warriors, also the palisade, fighting platforms, gates, and towers were too strong you would be assailed from above while trying to attack the gate or fence and be lucky to stay alive, no Wigson was in no doubt you would not shift these bastards in a hurry not without some trick to gain access. "We are here," said Berg,

THE BETRAYAL

Wigson looked up to the timber hall, wooden steps led up to the raised hall, poles with the flags of Bjorn fluttered in the winds, dragon head carvings adorned the wooden panels at the entrance to the hall.

WIGSON WAS IMPRESSED the hall was very large and ornate with runes and carvings. Wigson followed Berg up the steps followed by the two warriors that had arrived with Berg. A further two warriors with large doubled-headed axes stood guard at the top of the steps. Berg turned to Wigson " If you could give all your weapons to the guards, please, no visitor is allowed access to the Jarl armed" Wigson passed over his axe, sword, and seax his shield and bow where with his horse, he still had his small sharp killing blade tucked in his boot. He stepped to enter the hall and Berg spoke once more " The small blade you carry? My brother advised me of it as the handle was intricately carved, he noticed it when you all ate last night"

Wigson smiled but inwardly cursed he would be totally unarmed now "My eating knife," he said, "I did not think that as a weapon" he bent and retrieved the knife from his boot passing it to Berg. Berg turned the blade in his hand "A sea serpent by the look of the carving, very nice" he placed the blade with the other items and motioned Wigson to follow him inside.

The room was very large four large cooking fires were placed down the middle of the room with slaves busy at them, rows of benches ran down the full length of the room down each side, most were filled with warriors at the far a further long table ran the width of the hall on a raised platform, it was here that Wigson could see Jarl Bjorn, his son Healfden, a beautiful woman probably the Jarls wife thought Wigson, a strange bent man wrapped in rags and two strong looking seasoned warriors.

As Berg led Wigson down past the rows of warriors, the jeers and threats started some even threw food and stepped in Wigson's way to impede him laughing at him and poking him, Wigson just smiled and kept slowly pushing forward. A shout startled him "Enough" The Jarl stood and waved his arm the warriors went quiet and sat down to let Berg pass with Wigson smiling as he followed on. Wigson noticed a smaller table and bench just to the right below the raised platform at which Bjorn sat, Berg directed Wigson to sit at the bench then moved to stand at the side with his sword drawn. Wigson was unsure if Berg was his protector against the other warriors or the man who would strike him down if this meeting offended Jarl Bjorn. A slave appeared with ale, bread, and a trencher of meats and cheese, Jarl Bjorn looked down and nodded at Wigson, "Eat, drink refresh yourself we will talk in a while"

Wigson stood and nodded his head at Bjorn "My thanks Jarl, this looks tasty" he sat down and was soon tucking into the warm meat and tasty bread, the cheese was not bad too. Wigson gulped down some ale it was a bit tart he knew he had not been given some poor ale but well it was all free he should not grumble. The hall was hot raucous and very noisy, as he ate Wigson looked around at groups of warriors around the hall arm wrestled, had lifting, jumping, knife, and axe throwing competitions, sometimes things went too far, and fights broke out there was always someone pulling men apart and slapping them on the back passing ale skins around to calm them down. Wigson could not help but admire the comradeship of the men they all knew each other, and it was obvious from watching them they would readily fight and die for their Jarl and each other, a formidable force if he ever saw one. Wigson if he was true to himself was slightly jealous of all the Kings, Lords, and warriors he had fought with he had never felt or seen such a brotherhood. The evening drew on and Wigson had not noticed that Jarl Bjorn had left the Hall, he only became aware when Berg tapped his shoulder and motioned for him to follow. Berg walked up the steps to the far-left corner of the raised platform, pulling open a wooden door he stepped to the side and allowed Wigson to pass him, the room was small and contained a large wooden desk behind in a large ornate chair sat Jarl Bjorn the two large warriors stood either

THE BETRAYAL

side of him. Wigson nodded his head once more to the Jarl and stood silently waiting for it did not do well to speak before being invited to do so.

"Speak Wigson, friend of our friend Lavos," said Bjorn in a deep gruff voice

"Thank you, my lord, captain Lavos has requested a venture to you with a proposal" started Wigson.

Bjorn lifted a hand " Why should I do more, Lavos assured me that when I attacked, raped, and killed at Crag Rock he could force the warriors to turn on the Thane meaning I would have supporters between myself and King Offa, I take that with your arrival and request to speak with me this has not occurred"

Wigson paused and stood looking straight at Bjorn " You are a wise Lord, and correct, but we had a problem beyond our control"

Bjorn stood and slammed his meaty fists on the table rocking the lit tallow candles "That is not my issue friend Wigson" he shouted with a hiss of threat.

WIGSON TOOK a step backward but felt the closeness of the warrior Berg. Wigson stood and composed himself " My Thane Eldrig arranged at the last minute for the three warriors to be posted on sentry at the old watchtower therefore they were not at Crag Rock when you assaulted the farmsteads" he drew breath wanting to continue "But captain Lavos has an idea. He has been sent by the Thane to track you and your warriors and the three men will be with us he plans to have them on sentry duty at the forest on the edge of Lythe Valley" he waited for Jarl Bjorn to respond. Jarl Bjorn looked at his stern warriors and then back at Wigson "Why do you not just kill these three men I hear they are all old having around fifty summers each they should not be difficult to kill."

Wigson looked at the Jarl " You are correct, they are old but confident, loyal, and well-liked they could cause serious problems for Lavos when he makes his move, if they are not dealt with, he cannot be assured he will be your anchor against the King and Ealdormen to the north of us" once more Wigson paused and waited.

Jarl Bjorn drew the two warriors in to talk quietly they spoke in Danish and Wigson could only catch snippets one warrior could be heard to say, "Kill Him" and smiled as he said it. Jarl Bjorn even smiled at this, though shook his head.

All the time Wigson stood nervously by the sweat that was running down his face and back, he just wanted to be away from here and back on the road, why did Lavos have to complicate everything he thought?

Jarl Bjorn stood straight his two warriors stepping back " I have decided friend Wigson"

Wigson could feel his legs shaking, here we go he said to himself.

CHAPTER 7
THE DEATHS

The dozen warriors and Captain Lavos headed into the woods. Lavos and Wigson were the only two aware that the trap had been set for this very spot. The wood had a small clearing in it with large old rocks. It was here that they would make camp for the night and Lavos hoped oh how he hoped that the outcome would be favourable. The men had spent the last hours tracking the raiders and hunting trapping food to eat that night, Lavos was not worried about having a fire or two burning to cook the freshly caught animals, why would he be he was well aware of who and what was out there he smiled to himself once more.

LAVOS SHOWED his usual cruel hard nature by choosing three men to stand the first watch no point wasting decent fresh food filling their bellies they would soon be filled anyway. Raulf, Alun, and Trevik walked away from the camp and the other warriors as they prepared the food and the fires. "Well lads nothing fucking new sentry duty again and I can guarantee we will be stood here half the night if not all of it" spoke Raulf to his two loyal companions

Wigson had just been entering the camp unknown to the others he had slipped off to make sure that Jarl Bjorn and his warriors were nearby, He nodded to Raulf as he passed but he too had his own thoughts, not tonight friend Raulf, no not tonight. Tonight will be your last on sentry duty and the last with your stupid bullish friends, make the most of your jokes while you can.

As the three men approached the trees Raulf looked at his two lifelong friends, all three had served the Thane and his father before him, Raulf had been the lead warrior under the old captain his uncle Rhernhard a proper tough old bastard it was he that had trained Raulf, Trevik and Alun and imbodied the loyalty they had to the Thane and his family.

THE THREE MEN had their usual jokes and jibes at each other and the company they were keeping but soon set about the routine of sentries walking around the camp perimeter. It was a dark quiet night as the three stepped out among the trees all walking a route around the camp crossing each other but not following the same path. The old hands such as these had not lived this long without taking precautions.

Alun had passed both Trevik and then Raulf as he turned once more heading to the south side of the camp, he felt the old tingle at the back of his neck that something was not quite well right.

ALUN SLOWED his pace and then quickly but silently turned and fast paced a dozen more steps to his right taking him deeper into the trees before turning and heading at an angle back along the path to the area he would have been walking.

Alun was sure he was not alone he slid two throwing knives from his shoulder strap with his left hand and his seax he drew with his right hand, though not as fast as when in his youth if the enemy were around two horse lengths in front of him he should be able to throw the two knives and draw a third before they closed on him. He was very proud of his knife skills and was deadly even now with both hands. Alun was also an exceptional shot with an arrow his powerful bow was across his back.

A SMALL SNAP of a twig stopped Alun in his tracks. He paused returning his seax to his belt he drew arrows stabbing the points into the soft earth in front of him crouching down he laid the throwing knives next to them then drew the bow from his back, someone was dying tonight. He slowed his breath concentrating on the area around him, he knew they were out there he was unsure how many but at least four would be his guess he could smell ale and sweat on them manure on another yes, the attack would come soon, and he Alun was ready. The first to die jumped down from a tree just in front and to his right the arrow took him in the throat before he had even touched the mossy ground from the tree. The second came from his left and Alun dropped him with two arrows the thick cloak he wore had lessened the impact and the first arrow to his chest had not stopped him Alun fired more arrows quickly as two more charged at him from the front. The left man staggered and fell the fourth had a small shield and deflected the arrow. Alun's death came from behind he was too slow to turn it was manure man he only smelt his approach at the last minute and the man's blade came high into Alun's left side punching up through his ribs and piercing his heart, Alun quickly died a small sigh as his last breath left his body and all was quiet once more in the woods.

TREVIK WAS unaware of what had happened to his old friend Alun he was the furthest point from him and had not heard a sound, but he had started to feel uncomfortable these last moments at first, he had said to himself " You are getting old, Trevik the bear, jumping like a youth at shadows."

But was he? Now it was that old back of the neck tingling sensation, that one when you would say the hairs on your neck stood up, Trevik had stalked enemies himself before in the dead of night, he knew oh yes, he knew he was the one they were after whoever they where he was the one stalked tonight, he smiled he was ready for them they would not find him an easy target. He quickly thought of his two remaining friends Alun and Raulf well if tonight was there last night, they would be company aplenty for them he would take his share with him as he knew they would. Trevik silently pulled the doubled-headed axe from across his shoulders looping the leather strap around his right wrist, from his belt he drew a smaller axe just as deadly this had a small sharp blade and a long steel point that he could smash through chainmail deep into any willing soft flesh.

TREVIK SLOWED his pace and his breathing rolling his shoulders to loosen his muscles. He stepped out between the trees into a small circle of light breaking through from the moon. Trevik was no small man tall and broad across the shoulders he had once for a gamble lifted three men above his head to win some ale, he had long greying hair and beard and with the bearskin cloak he wore he had the appearance of a large bear. He stood in the waning moonlight waiting, no point in running he would let them come to him and save his energy.

HE HEARD the rustle of leaves, and the creak of branches and shrubs as they were pushed apart to allow access through, he could smell the sweat and stench of horses upon his attackers they kept stopping they were nervous. Trevik closed his eyes controlled his heart rate breathing and staying relaxed was a reason he had stayed alive so long. The attack came the first man from the left a sword and shield in his hand quickly followed by a second running fast straight in front of him, he would reach Trevik first, the man running held a boar spear the head bright and polished aiming for Treviks chest. Trevik spun quickly to his left turning away from the boar spear as the man drew level Trevik swung the doubled-head axe into the back of his neck blood sprayed up Treviks arm and the man dropped instantly to the floor dead. Trevik had noticed a third man appear from his right, he would wait, for as Trevik had hacked into the neck of the first the spin he had actioned drew him closer to the first man Trevik raised his small axe and with a mighty force slammed the spike down into his head the point came out in his mouth blood gushing down his chest, two down. Trevik ducked as he noticed a fourth man half hidden in the bushes, he fired an arrow which took the third man who was now behind Trevik in the throat, Trevik drew a throwing knife from his belt quickly letting it fly at the archer, the archer half turned to dodge the blade but was slow and it skimmed over his cheek and across his eye, the archer turned and ran.

A BELLOW to Treviks right saw a fifth man appear an axe in his hand he was only slightly smaller in stature than him Trevik smiled now this could be good. The two men were evenly matched, both attacked using two axe's sparks flew as the blades spun and caught against each other. Trevik drew first blood a line across his attacker's right arm, he slammed the spike into the already wounded arm to render his attacker only one useful arm. The man growled he was not out of the fight, yet he threw the axe catching Treviks shoulder and snapping the bone, grabbing another axe from his belt he charged Trevik who swung his double-headed axe straight into the man's stomach "Great fight." He spluttered through the blood from his mouth. Trevik looked at him as he died "I was lucky" he replied.

TREVIK STOOD and looked around his right shoulder was in agony, but he had downed four men and wounded a fifth he needed to locate Raulf and Alun if they both still lived. Collecting his weapons and grabbing the boar spear he set off to assist his friends little knowing that Alun lay dead just across the trees from him.

Trevik was unaware that Rauf had found their friend and was even now heading to find Trevik, both men heading to one final battle against the enemy. Both men knew the enemy where nearby and closing in Raulf hoped he could reach Trevik before he was attacked. Raulf watched as from the darkness appearing like horned-armed demons four shadows grew and crept towards him. This was it. They were searching for him or Trevik or probably both. Time slowed at that moment he could see the slow lumbering gait of the men as they drew closer to him, his breathing slow and shallow, and his heart had slowed too as if waiting to beat fast and hard when the attack eventually came.

He was sure they did not see him or sense him, he saw the first man and moved to step from the tree's shelter to make his attack his axe held high to take the man through the neck, suddenly a dark shape shouting and growling shot from the undergrowth swinging his sword wildly the first man ducked and spun to Treviks left in a blur of movement yet graceful and with speed like a dancer twirling around. Trevik took two more steps away from the warrior half turning his face to look upon his killer and suddenly fell to his knees his guts sliced open quickly spilling over his belt and trousers the gore running onto his legs and leafy grass in front of him.

Trevik looked up at the men "Treacherous bloody scum " he said as he made eye contact with his killer.

A knife sliced quickly across his throat ending the proud warrior's life in an instant.

It was then that Raulf stepped from the shadows of the tree his face a mask of anger and upset he stepped towards the four warriors calm and content he would be reunited soon with his loyal friends.

"Hello dark scum, it's time to tackle the old lion now, let's dance"

A voice deep and dark responded, "Old lion, mongrel lame dog more like, lets fucking finish this once and for all men, these three bloody turds always thought themselves elite and better than the rest of us, we have proven them wrong now, chopped them down to size what say you men."

Suddenly more shapes stepped out from the darkness of the trees to surround the proud Raulf stood alone in defiance. The warriors all rushed forward at once to throw a circle around him. Raulf laughed and thought to himself no escape this time then. Calmly Raulf readied himself for the attack, then with a blur of speed as in his younger years he spun, he turned, he jumped, he twisted and ducked as he danced around the swords, spears, and axes that reached out to end his life here in the trees. He stabbed and swung both his seax and axe the first one fell his head split by the axe exploding like some overripe fruit the second had his sword arm taken from the elbow blood pumping everywhere as he bled out, blades struck home on Raulf's body, cuts, nicks on his arms and torso he was tiring each cut slowed him further, the blood flowed from his wounds sapping his strength. He took his last soul to join him in his journey the seax stuck in his attacker's eye.

RAULF LOOKED AROUND and his attackers, why did the grinning loud idiot look so tall? It was then he realized he was lying on his back dying.

"Dirty bloody scum,"

Raulf smiled to himself as his life slowly ebbed away, he once more saw the smiling face of Sareen as she played in the yard by the old barn with his family and friends, he thought of the dead raiders about him, he had served out his justice, he was content.

CHAPTER 8
THE KING'S MEETING

Thane Eldrig and his daughter Eleen were distraught when Captain Lavos returned with the bodies of Raulf, Trevik, and Alun days later. Eleen visibly shook her body, as she sobbed in open grief these three men had been constant at the side of the ruling family Trevik had even taught her to use a bow and axe while Alun had shown her how to use a knife, he had even gifted her one with a smooth oak handle with carvings of flowers perfectly balanced for her she still wore it now strapped to her leg under her dress. Raulf was her tutor for years not only with swords but with family history and dealing with visiting traders and merchants. Oh, how she would miss them, her elderly maid Ethane stood by her side hugging Eleen she too wept as she had been very close to Trevik they had been friends for years and even lovers in their youth.

ELEEN COULD HEAR her father shouting and throwing items around the hall, she glanced across at Lavos with tear-filled eyes, he stood grim-faced with a steely glint in his own eyes, he turned at one point to his junior Wigson and a curl of a smile crossed his face. Eleen was unsure what was happening, but she would speak privately with her father later. Her father like she was angry and upset they had lost three good warriors and not solved the issue of the raiders instead they had come back with news that the host of raiders was a much larger force than presumed and with a secure walled settlement. Lavos had agreed with Wigson to provide some information to Eldrig about the size of the settlement, walls, towers, and gate and how many men he had seen they supplied this saying that Wigson had followed the attacking raiders to find their lair.

Enough "Lavos you and your man are dismissed " shouted Eldrig

"My Thane But..." Lavos started to reply "I SAID ENOUGH" interrupted Eldrig. "NOW LEAVE MY HALL" he pointed to the door as he said it.

Lavos and Wigson turned and left the hall, slamming the door behind him Lavos smiled at Wigson soon my friend soon, he will not last much longer we just need to push him a little more his health is already failing we are nearing the end of this, and we will succeed. The door opened behind Lavos who quickly went quiet it was Ethane who appeared from the door, she nodded her head " Captain, I am away to fetch some food for our Thane and Eleen" Lavos stepped to the side "The news of my failure has upset our Thane, I am hopeful he will be okay" then he stepped away with Wigson in tow.

Eldrig sat in his private room with his head in his hands he quietly sobbed he would miss Raulf greatly the man had been steadfast and loyal why he had taught Eldrig all he knew about fighting and ruling the family had supported the Thane's before him for generations and now the bloodline was all but extinct, just one survived a cousin of Raulf's but he was a senior man at arms for Lord Ludeca who was Eldrig's liege lord, Bern was his name Eldrig did not even know if Bern had any family of his own, but he must be told as Crag Rock was now his.

. . .

Eldrig looked up as Ethane entered with some bread, cheese, and fruit for Eleen and him, she placed the platter down and went to leave, "Ethane sit with us and join with us as we talk and celebrate the lives of Raulf, Trevik, and Alun, these men whereas close to you as ourselves"

Ethane looked at her Thane and pulled a small stool to the table "My thanks, I shall serve us"

The three joined in grief ate the bread and cheese and drank some of the ale in silence. Eldrig looked at Ethane and spoke "Ethane could you ask Hardison, Loff, Aruth, Ceolstan, Thrun, and Wareson to have horses saddled for themselves and both mine and Eleen's too"

Ethane stood "My Thane" leaving the room she looked back at Eleen with a questioning look.

Eleen walked around the table and hugged her father "What is your plan?" she asked. Eldrig looked up "We go to seek King Offa; I need to speak with Lord Ludeca we need help, and I must speak with him about the raiders, Raulf, and Crag Rock"

The next morning Eldrig set off with his small band of warriors he sent the hunter twins Hardison and Loff out in front then he and Eleen were riding in the middle of Aruth and Ceolstan while Thrun along with Wareson who brought up the rear. Eldrig had argued again with Lavos this morning he was full of mistrust for his captain, and he had left his steward Rolf in charge. The group headed north following for the main part of the old Roman road. Each evening they stopped at small villages or in the ruins of some of the old Roman buildings and forts.

The journey was slow as Eldrig was not used to long hours on a horse, they did not go hungry as the twins hunted each day as they travelled, a banquet of hare, pigeons, and sometimes fish or snake along with berries and roots made up the evening meal. On the third day as they closed on Lord Ludeca' s lands. Aruth stopped the group suddenly he could see Loff heading back towards them at speed it was too early in the day to be making camp. Eldrig moved to Aruth's side "What do you see" Aruth looked at his Thane "It is Loff, he is approaching fast which I find strange"

Eldrig looked at Aruth " We will wait here and see what is wrong, Aruth if things go wrong you take my daughter and ride you stop for nothing, do you understand me"

Aruth nodded "Yes, my Thane, I know my duty Raulf taught all of us well, we will not let you down"

Moments later Loff was at Eldrig's side " It is the King" was all he said.

Eldrig and the others watched as a large body of men crested the hill King Offa's banner fluttered in the wind. Eldrig sagged in his saddle he had found his King and by the look of it his liege lord was as usual with the King. Eldrig climbed down from his horse along with Eleen as the King approached, Ealdorman Ludeca smiled at him from his huge horse "Eldrig, what are you doing riding the open lands, what irks you, my man"

Eldrig bowed his head to King Offa and Ludeca " My King, My Lord we are troubled with a large group of raiders, and I lack the men to defend our people I seek help from you"

King Offa looked at him and turned to his men " Oswi, we will camp here for the night set the squires and new warriors to get my tent up and food" Oswi replied quickly "Yes, My King" he turned to give the orders to the troop of men. King Offa spoke again to Eldrig " We will speak later of this, attend my tent later. We can eat and discuss the problem" Without waiting for a reply he turned and rode away. Ludeca looked at Eldrig "The King has a lot to deal with at this time raiders approach all our borders as do the Welsh, I will try my best to support you my old friend" Eldrig nodded "Thank you Ealdorman Ludeca. Is that old dog Bern with you still, if so could you bring him with you I need to speak with him too" Ludeca smiled " Aye he still serves me well, he trains our new troops alongside my son Oswi, they will both be there."

. . .

Later that evening Thane Eldrig and Eleen walked across the King's campsite to his tent Aruth and Ceolstan escorted them through the camp. The King's men and Lord's household troops all sat around small campfires eating and drinking, some sat cleaning weapons and armour. Eleen had never seen such a motley crew, a huge range of weapons, armour, lots of the men carried scars and old injuries and were obviously used to fighting for their King.

Two guards stood outside the King's tent and a younger warrior in gleaming chainmail he smiled as Eldrig, and Eleen approached.

"Good evening is it Thane Eldrig he enquired.

"It is, yes and you are?" replied Eldrig "I am Oswi, son of Ludeca, and is this your daughter Eleen?"

Eleen nodded a reply " I am yes, Lord Oswi" Oswi smiled and laughed "Thank you for the honour you bestowed me unfortunately I am the third son to my father Ealdorman Ludeca, and therefore plain Oswi warrior to the King and trainer to his new troops and squires"

Eleen laughed " We all start somewhere Oswi if you would show my father and I in please"

Oswi pulled aside the large curtain to allow Eldrig and Eleen access into the large tent, the King sat in a chair at the far end and a fire smoked in the middle leaving the air inside the tent warm and stuffy the smoke lingered making the tent dark and gloomy.

The Lords and senior warriors sat in a half circle on either side of the King, a chest with a blanket thrown over it stood empty, and it was here that Oswi directed Eldrig and Eleen to sit. Servants attended them with drinks and Oswi stood respectfully behind them.

Ealdorman Ludeca spoke first "My Lord King, we are all here, now"

"My thanks Ludeca" replied Offa, "Thane Eldrig, is here to seek assistance for a problem with the raider scum, Eldrig if you could let us know the issues you are having"

Eldrig stood "Thank you my Lord King, my Lords, we have been struggling for many months with raiders attacking our outlying settlements, until recently we only had cattle and winter food stores stolen. But last week a large party sailed upriver and attacked Crag Rock, a small farming settlement rich fertile land and occupied by a family of great hunters and farmers, My Lord King your man at arms Bern it is his own family that farms and owns this land."

Offa looked across at Bern "Bern I feel this could involve you personally, take a seat my old friend we will learn of the problems and make a plan, be assured I will involve you in it if revenge is required"

Bern grabbed an old barrel and sat next to Thane Eldrig. "Thank you, Sire"

Offa nodded at Bern and looked across at Eldrig once more "Pray continue"

Eldrig nodded once more and continued " The attack was particularly brutal, all the men folk were slain and the women and young girls all raped then killed. Stored crops and foods were burnt and stolen. The whole settlement was set aflame." Eldrig paused to draw breath and take a drink, Eleen reached up and touched her father's hand. Eldrig turned back to his King " The leader of this small settlement was an old warrior and tutor of our family Raulf nephew to our old captain Rhernhard and family to your esteemed warrior Bern" Eldrig looked at Bern at this point, he was sat grim-faced learning of the destruction of his old settlement from his childhood and youth.

Eldrig continued talking of how he had set a band of his warriors to track and kill the raiders, the King and Lords nodded in agreement to him. Bern's face was set as stone when he learned of Raulf and his brother warrior's deaths. Oswi had stepped close and rested his hand on his old tutor's shoulder. Oswi could feel his old friend was tense and angry he had met Raulf himself on a few occasions and knew him to be a first-class warrior.

Oswi continued to listen as Thane Eldrig provided information about the location and number of warriors at the raider's settlement. King Offa was listening intently to Eldrig asking questions and speaking with the Lords and warriors around him. Oswi saw Eldrig sag as he sat down on the chest physically drained from the experience. Oswi noticed Eleen gripping her father's hand once more in comfort he was drawn to her beauty, he could see how she cared for those around her. Oswi became aware that King Offa was talking directly to him. "I am sorry, My King I missed that I was thinking of my old friend Bern and his family"

King Offa looked at Oswi "So I could see" Oswi blushed, and the other lords and warriors smiled they had all seen him looking at Eleen.

King Offa Continued " Now we have your attention Oswi you will lead a detachment of men Alfe, Bergad, Brune, Egbert, Ethelbert, Edhert, Ren, Strum, Dristan, Thornstan, Wigstan, Winebert the warriors you are instructing you may take Bern with you as your second and senior warrior, take your squires and the gaggle training under them some hard work will put some meat on their bones"

The other warriors and Lords laughed at the discomfort the squires in training would endure.

The King looked at Ealdorman Ludeca "Ludeca could you spare three experienced warriors to assist Bern with the training?"

Lord Ludeca smiled he was grateful for the opportunity the King had provided his youngest son his small independent command

"Of course, he can take Hern, Ludic, Wulfure, they are all old comrades of Bern and Oswi knows them well, they are all experienced and will be of valued assistance."

"Good, good that is that settled then" replied King Offa he stepped down from his chair and approached Bern "Bern, our trusted warrior and trainer of men, we are sorry for the loss of your family, as the senior male left we will arrange that the settlement is rebuilt and you are made leader of Crag Rock, I give permission for you to move your wife, children and their families to the land to serve Thane Eldrig and my kingdom, I feel your loss I remember in my youth meeting Raulf he took me out hunting boar along with his men, I fell from my horse when the boar startled me, it fell dead mere inches from my feet moments later it had a spear in its right shoulder, and arrow it its right eye and a small axe in its head I turned to see Raulf, Trevik and Alun stood behind me all looking serious Raulf spoke to me " Our thanks my prince for providing us an easy target for the boar that was very brave of you" I remember us all laughing after that, it was not brave of me and they knew it but they kept me alive and did not chastise or embarrass me, I learned to stay on my horse when hunting boar after that"

Bern looked up at his king "My thanks for the honour you do Raulf and my family, I will do as you request, and we will ensure Crag Rock rises from the ashes to continue serving you and the Kingdom."

CHAPTER 9
THE TRAINING

The next morning Ealdorman Ludeca said farewell to his son Oswi who was mounted with Bern and his troop of warriors and squires along with Thane Eldrig, Eleen, and his warriors. "Take care my son, see to the Thane's settlement and assist him in keeping control of his village from the raiders, I will see you soon the King wishes to turn south and see if he can attack some of the raiders, I have sent a message south to some of the southern Lords and Ealdormen seeking assistance on behalf of the King"

Oswi smiled at his father "Yes sir I will uphold the Kings request, to strengthen Farndon and start the rebuild of Crag Rock, so Bern can resettle it"

EALDORMAN LUDECA CLIMBED upon his horse and galloped south after his King. Oswi turned to Bern "Come my old friend let's get going, we have a ride to Farndon"

Bern nodded "Yes, let us be away," he replied.

. . .

THE BETRAYAL

THE JOURNEY back to Farndon was uneventful. Oswi and Bern kept the troops in good order and during the journey took small groups of them out to train on scouting and fieldcraft, Bern was a stern and serious instructor but believed all troops should be aware of how to hunt, search, scout, and follow tracks. Oswi rode with Thane Eldrig and Eleen and spoke to Eldrig regards the condition of the walls around Farndon and the state of the road and bridge. It was obvious that a lot of work needed to be done to maintain it all Oswi knew they would be busy.

IN PRIVATE CONVERSATIONS Eleen informed Oswi of her distrust of Captain Lavos and the core group of warriors he kept close to him. Oswi knew he would have to be careful. The captain would not like that he and the others had been sent by the king to improve things. Once the group was close to nearing Farndon Eldrig sent his personal warriors out in front to make sure his steward Rolf was aware and also to inform Captain Lavos. Oswi had decided that his troop of warriors would make camp at Crag Rock they could clear away an area and make a weapons exercise yard to continue training the men. Then they could also build a new barn and home for Bern's family who would hopefully arrive in the coming weeks. It would help strengthen and condition the men for the use of fighting in mail with shields, swords, and axes.

Oswi had discussed with Eldrig that Bern and his father's household troops would be the only warriors to attend him at his hall, Oswi hoped that this would then not offend Lavos too much, though both agreed once some initial repairs had taken place at Crag Rock, they would need to look at Farndon.

The group stopped at Crag Rock the charred timbers still stood dark and twisted stark reminders of the destruction wrought on the settlement. Bern climbed from his horse and walked through the middle of the open yard looking at the destruction. Oswi could see that his long-time friend and mentor was physically and emotionally affected by the scene. Oswi climbed down from his horse and stepped towards Bern.

BERN TURNED and looked at his former student " I am okay Oswi, Let's get to it, I will task the squires to set up some tents for the men then see to the horses, if you wish to task the men to start clearing the areas" Oswi used to instructions from his mentor nodded in understanding and both went to the tasks.

Oswi first walked to Eldrig and Eleen "Thane Eldrig, Eleen, I trust you are safe to complete the journey to Farndon, I will set the men here to task and we will call this evening to speak with you and Captain Lavos."

Eldrig nodded and moved his horse forward, Eleen smiled at Oswi "Thank you" was all she said and followed her father.

Oswi stood watching her ride away listening to the shouting and bawling of Bern to the squires.

Oswi smiled and walked to the troops, he instructed his own fathers' troops to arrange a guard and picket the troop's horses while he set the warriors to hauling hulks of timbers and clearing the area for the camp and training area.

Aruth arrived at Crag Rock the next morning, trudging on behind him where three carts, two loaded with planks and freshly felled trees, the third plied with tools, ropes, cords, iron rings, and nails. Oswi and Bern already awake and discussing the plan to rebuild stood watching as they all so noticed a steady stream of men and youths behind the carts.

Aruth climbed from the lead cart " Good Morning, My Lady Eleen requested that we attend with the supplies and bring men to assist with the building of Crag Rock."

Oswi clapped Bern on the back "My old friend shall we get started on Crag Rock"

Bern smiled "Our thanks Aruth, we have an area cleared to start the build so we can set to work straight away"

Oswi and Bern tasked the warriors to unload the timbers from the carts, while Aruth passed instructions to the menfolk and youths.

Two huge-looking men approached Oswi the first towered over him with long black hair tied back, a long beard hands the size of a shovel, and massive scared muscled arms. The second was slightly smaller but definitely wider and had a huge paunch of a belly.

The bearded giant spoke first "My Lord I am Brak the smith I have some experience with building and preparing the ground to support structures Thane Eldrig has sent me to task the men to build the frames and foundations"

Oswi smiled up at Brak " Our thanks Brak, we had planned to have a large barn over to the right with two floors if possible and then running at a right angle to it a large communal hall for the troops a third building here where we stand which will be for Bern and his family and as more arrive, we will build additional buildings to form them into a square with a central yard. The doors will all be inside the yard and any windows on the outer wall need to be high up we will eventually build stone and mud walls to link the buildings and a gateway at the corner here of the barn and Bern's home."

Brak turned to survey the area quickly and nodded, "I agree but I would advise losing some of the fields, making an area between them and the buildings to better see the approach of anyone, I will set to work digging the holes for the supporting posts" with that he turned and left.

The second smiled at Oswi "And I sir am Gava the butcher, Thane Eldrig has provided meat and vegetables so I might cook some tasty warm food for everyone to eat later"

Oswi grinned he had been eating poor food cooked by the squires so a decent meal would be welcome. "That sounds fabulous Gava, I will leave you to the meal then."

Gava nodded and turned ushering some women to assist with the preparation and set the fires burning to cook the food.

. . .

As the sun began to set Aruth and the menfolk along with Brak and Gava set off home. Bern stood in what would be the large open yard looking around the barn had its supports in place and a foundation of stone and mud on which some planks had now been fitted. The large communal hall had its base structure and supports, Bern's own home was partly built like the barn. He smiled as he looked at Oswi "It is looking great already, my friend, tomorrow we will split the men half to continue with the building half to start training we cannot afford for the men not to be prepared for battle."

The next few days Bern and Oswi tasked the men, half of those buildings, to haul logs and planks, stones, and mud from the river. Built small walls and hoisted timbers and planks up to create the walls of the buildings each evening the men ached but built up their strength and stamina which they did not at first realize was assisting with their training. The warriors tasked to train in the art of war had mock battles and formation training using sword and shield, axe, spear, hand-to-hand fighting, archery, and horsemanship, the men strained at the weapons, limbs ached, bodies battered and bruised.

The squires were set to tasks and learn too no man or youth fell short when Bern was around training troops. The squires learned to repair chainmail and leather armour, cook, tend the horses, and how forage and trap food. Bern drove all of them hard, but he took pride in knowing that this troop of men would be strong and fast in a battle and would serve his lord's son Oswi well and be a troop he could be proud of and rely on.

Bern had trained many men for his lord and King over the years and had turned out some skilled men to assist with keeping Mercia safe. Bern headed back to the yard to check how today's training was going he had left the two section leaders in charge, and they were practicing with the spears today throwing them also attack and defend while on foot. Bern was surprised when he arrived to find the men sat in a group deep in conversation, Bern stormed over "What the bloody hell is going on here, are you all children sitting around with nothing to do

The two section leaders jumped up. Edhert and Ren looked at each other Ren spoke first " We are having a discussion about the spears Bern"

"Oh, pray enlighten me my valued and experienced warriors" replied Bern"

Ren nudged Edhert and nodded his head.

Edhert visibly gulped he may be in charge of a group of warriors, but nobody liked to try and look better than Bern it was not good to try.

"Well, we have been training with the spears and launching them at the wooden posts and well we found that they bend, and we struggle to pull them free and then they need to be repaired" Edhert looked at Bern who nodded for him to continue. "Yes so, we looked to strengthen the pole making it longer and if we make the head of the spear broader and shaped so it tapers on four edges this would make the tip sharper like an arrow, but if we fasten a metal bar at the top of the pole just behind the head it would stop the head going too deep and should release easier also if the tip is tapered like the arrow heads it should be sharper to penetrate leather jerkins and chain mail but again should be easy to pull free" Edhert was in full flow now, Bern listened carefully to the explanations, he raised his hand to halt Edhert "That is all good and yes it may work but to what advantage once we throw the spears it will still be shield, sword and axe time" Edhert nodded "Yes normally but with the extra length of the pole we think we could use it from horse back to charge a line of warriors, stabbing down with the spear as we ride by the spear should pull free to allow us to reform and charge them again. It would be useful if we were fighting a larger body of men as we could thin them down before we have to fight man on man or shield wall to shield wall" Edhert finished he looked at Ren and then the other warriors standing silent now waiting for Bern.

He turned and walked away the men all watching his back as he walked away.

Bern stopped and shouted over his shoulder, "Edhert, Ren go speak with Brak the smith explain your idea see what he thinks if he can make it ask him about the best shape and metal and wood for the shaft, then ask if he could make twenty of them if he agrees ask him a price, then barter with him to get it lower" He stepped out once more " Get going lads, the rest of you back to training"

Bern smiled as he walked away hearing the men groan, yes, he was proud of this bunch they were learning and thinking as a unit and looking to better their skills and thinking of ideas. Bern would never admit to them he was proud of them. Bern went to find Oswi to inform him of how the training was going. Bern watched Edhert and Ren ride away then looked over at Oswi and could see him in conversation with Lady Eleen, Bern had not seen her return to Farndon, she was escorted by the twin hunters it looked like they had been successful while out as a deer along with various birds hung over one saddle and across the packhorse hung a boar and hares.

Eleen turned as Bern approached "Good to see you Bern, I was just here to invite both you and Oswi to my father's hall tonight for a feast, we are so happy how Crag Rock has progressed, and Father thinks it is time to improve the troops and defences at Farndon now as per the Kings wishes"

Bern looked at Oswi who was smiling as Eleen spoke oh great, he said to himself the lad is smitten with her.

Bern nodded " That would be nice My Lady, we will see you later, today, can I drag the young sir away from you to inspect our troops"

Eleen smiled "Of course, we will see you later." She turned with a swish of her skirts climbing onto her dappled palfrey waving as she turned and headed back to Farndon.

Oswi turned to Bern "How are we doing, my old friend." Bern raised his eyebrows "With what?" he replied Oswi smiled "The training of course my old friend the training what else." Bern kept a stern face "Less of the old you, young pup." Laughing he turned "Come on Oswi we will walk to the river through the fields, and I will tell you how the training goes and what the men have devised under Edhert and Ren"

The two men's mentor and leader walked through the yard Bern pointing at individual men and advising of the skills and merits of each one and where additional training was required. Oswi was always surprised how Bern remembered every warrior and squire's name, how he knew the skills each man had, and where they needed more training. The two men walked on as Bern chatted away he needed to strengthen his arms, or he would not survive a shield wall, he needed more time to sit upon a horse, he keeps falling off. Oswi knew the men's names, and Bern knew each man personally.

CHAPTER 10
THE ATTACK

Oswi and Bern sat at the top table along with Thane Eldrig, Eleen, and Captain Lavos. Bern had taken an instant distrust of the captain he just well he did not like him he was like a cornered animal looking and watching all the time, no Bern knew he was part of the problem here in Farndon time would tell.

Oswi was deep in conversation with Thane Eldrig and Eleen, they were discussing the current layout of the hall and buildings inside the wall and the troops Thane Eldrig had at his disposal. Eleen was talking about the old watchtower over the old Roman stone bridge and the condition it was currently in. Oswi agreed that this was a first line of defence for the river crossing and a vantage point to keep a check of the boats up and down the river. Eleen felt a chill run down her spine she turned slightly to feel the grim face of Lavos looking at her, she smiled at him and felt his eyes bore deep into her it felt like he was looking into her very soul, his lip curled in what passed as a smile from him.

THE BETRAYAL

. . .

Lavos was not impressed he had heard days before of the troop of men that Eldrig had returned with and knew now that his plans needed to change and adapt. He had only met the champion warrior Oswi this evening. Still, he hated him with a tremendous passion as all he had listened to from his Eleen was Oswi this, Oswi that, Oswi is a man of honour, Oswi is a great warrior, Oswi, Oswi, Oswi. Lavos seethed inside. Oswi would know pain soon, he could see that the snip of a man was in love with Eleen. He would show them both who the greater man was.

Oswi had felt the unmistakable distaste from Lavos when he met him Lavo's displeasure of him was truly overwhelming Oswi felt it cover him like a blanket, Oswi would speak with Bern later Lavos needed watching maybe Aruth and a couple of the other trusted warriors could provide some information on Lavos and keep an eye on him.

Wigson was at the hall that evening and had watched the young handsome warrior and his mentor arrive, Wigson saw strength of character in Oswi and instantly knew from seeing Bern that both would have exceptional fighting skills. Wigson was impressed with what he saw but also had doubt set in his mind they needed these two leaders of men and their troops away from Farndon. Lavos could not make his move on leadership with them hanging around the place. Wigson kept a watch on the group as they sat talking, pondering, thinking how he could advise Lavos.

Thane Eldrig talked with Oswi, and Eleen provided more information, the young warrior had been impeccably trained he knew the art of war both attack and defence, and understood the need for a strong base to sally from Farndon was far from that but listening to Oswi he was aware it could soon be a good stronghold. Eldrig was struggling with his health he had been for a few years but the ride to find his King had taken a toll on him, he was weak of limb, he could hardly eat, and he had spasms of pain in his chest and limbs. Eldrig was listening to Eleen talk of the watchtower and noticed how Oswi looked at Eleen and she at Oswi, he was pleasantly surprised but also pleased, he only hoped that he had the strength and means to live a while longer to try and seek a match from Oswi's father Ealdorman Ludeca after all Oswi was the youngest of three sons he would not inherit the Lord's title and lands. Eldrig smiled he could not have hoped for a better match and if the two had love for each other as Eldrig had once held for his own wife then so much the better, as he knew his only daughter would live a happy life.

THE NIGHT WAS SOON over and Oswi and Bern returned to Crag Rock both voiced their uncertainty of Lavos. The next few days went by quickly Crag Rock was nearing completion and Bern's wife with the two younger children turned up along with Bern's three grown-up sons and their own families and a few farming families that had worked with Bern's sons. Crag Rock was resettled Bern was a lot happier now.

OSWI along with Brak had started developing plans to strengthen the walls of Farndon and build a stronger gate with towers. Bern and Aruth were in conversation with them when a traveling merchant turned up flustered and shouting for Thane Eldrig for assistance.

The four men went out of the main area by the gate and stables, Wigson and two others of Lavos men were in deep conversation with the merchant. Oswi could see Eldrig's steward Rolf was trying to calm the situation down, Oswi looked at Bern and Aruth when he heard the words King, attack, and slaughter. The four of them quickened their pace towards the merchant they needed to get him inside Eldrig's hall and away from the eyes and ears of the people of Farndon before panic ensued. Bern and Aruth sensed what needed to be done and pushed roughly past Wigson and the others moving them to the side as Oswi quickly reached out touching the merchant on the arm he steered him away with quiet quick words "Come my friend let us find Thane Eldrig" Rolf quickly understood what Oswi was doing, and he too ushered the merchant along passed the startled people of Farndon and away from Wigson and the others. As Rolf and Oswi cajoled the merchant along Aruth, Brak, and Bern followed on. Bern caught a movement within the stable block and could see Lavos half in the shadows with a sneering smile across his face, Bern turned slightly to see Wigson's sly smile spread over his face. Bern had the feeling they had been set up, but why, he would inform Oswi after they had listened to the merchant.

Aruth saw the twins Hardison and Loff, he waved them over talking quickly he explained the situation and bade them stand guard at the door to the hall in the hope it would deter the townsfolk. Brak went back to his work, and Bern along with Aruth ventured into the hall Eldrig was pacing backwards and forwards along the raised platform Eleen stood shocked with her hands over her face, Rolf was stood taking notes and the merchant was visibly shaking as he regaled his tale of death and destruction, his loss of goods and wives, slaves. He told of a running battle with dead and dying men, horses, slaves, and young camp followers with heads split open like overripe fruit, guts, and entrails spilling the ground sodden with the blood of men. It was a grim tale to hear, Oswi continued to question him to gain some information of value as so far none had been given.

"My dear merchant please calm yourself, sir, please we need precise information from you so we can assist" The merchant looked at Oswi and sagged onto a nearby bench.

"And whom may you be sir to question me so is this not the hall of Thane Eldrig" sneered the merchant.

Oswi quickly replied, " It is so, I am Oswi, son of Ealdorman Ludeca I command a troop of King Offa's personal guard and I am charged to recruit and train new troops, My King has tasked me to support Thane Eldrig with the problem of raiders in the area."

The merchant laughed " I think the King would have appreciated your troops, as it was his men attacked. I was within the camp trading with the Ealdorman when the attack occurred. The attack was three days ago just south of the Old Roman Road. The King and his troops were attacked, and many killed I alone escaped from my own party, the raiders attacked quickly with speed and just before night most men had settled for the evening, I heard the clash of arms and the screams of the dying. The King and your father rallied the troops and made a fighting withdrawal. I believe they were trying to head to the Roman outpost further up the road" At this the merchant slumped onto the bench he looked drained.

Oswi looked to Bern and nodded, and Bern stepped forward drawing the merchant away so that Oswi could speak more discreetly with Thane Eldrig.

Bern was impressed with how Oswi had managed the panic-stricken merchant it must have been hard hearing that the attack could potentially have killed his father and his King. Bern spoke in whispers to Aruth.

"I feel that Oswi and I will be leaving soon my friend, I will speak plainly as we may have little time, I trust not Captain Lavos and his friend Wigson or the men who attach themselves as flies attract to shit." Aruth looked Bern in the eyes "I agree friend Bern, I agree, fear not if you leave then Hardison, Loff, Ceolstan, Thrun, Wareson along with myself will arrange a guard for Thane Eldrig and Eleen, I will also take the maid Ethane and Brak the smith into my confidence." Bern nodded "Will those men follow you?" he enquired

Aruth smiled "Do not worry Bern, my Thane appointed me the leader of that section as a reward for service, he tasked me to bring loyal men only to the group, I actually think his daughter Eleen had something to do with it, Brak will stand by me no matter what as he is a distant cousin to me he also hates Lavos who never wishes to pay for repairs to his personal weapons and equipment."

Bern nodded and the two watched Oswi in a heated argument with Thane Eldrig.

"No Oswi, I will not release you if raiders are out there you must bring all the troops here, we must abandon Crag Rock and secure Farndon those where the King's Orders, you must assist me" Thane Eldrig was beside himself he shouted, screamed, ranted at Oswi.

Oswi calmly stood by as Thane Eldrig stormed up and down shouting spittle flew from his mouth as he continued to rant and rave.

Oswi was stern but determined that there was a genuine need to support the King.

Thane Eldrig looked at Oswi we will discuss this further he turned to Aruth "Go and find Lavos and Wigson ask them to attend me here and we will discuss the merits"

Aruth turned and left the hall. Thane Eldrig looked to "Ethane please find some refreshments for us if you would"

Lavos and Wigson arrived, and Thane Eldrig waved the group around a communal table he sat at one end with Eleen Lavos and Wigson sat to his right, Oswi, Bern and Aruth sat opposite them, and Rolf sat to the far end, Ethane busied herself supplying drinks and food to all those sitting around.

Eldrig spoke to Rolf "Rolf please could you run through the information provided by our merchant friend"

Rolf quickly and efficiently ran through the situation of the attack for everyone, Lavos and Wigson gasped in surprise at the attack.

Thane Eldrig went through the situation though he was adamant that he and Farndon would not be involved, Lavos and Wigson both agreed with him and supported the argument to keep Oswi and his troops within Farndon.

Oswi calmly explained that he and his troops would be leaving to locate and support the King and that he and they were not under any leadership or authority of Thane Eldrig, Eleen calmly listened to the arguments she understood the worries of her father but also those of Oswi. These seemed uncertain times and action needed to be taken she drew breath and spoke.

"Father" Everyone paused the heated discussion and looked at Eleen

she started again "Father, I understand your concerns, but we have a duty to our Lord and King we must send troops to assist"

Thane Eldrig went mad he snarled at Eleen "You do not know of what you talk about begone to your chamber"

Eleen was furious and stormed out.

Lavos watched on, this was going well everyone was disagreeing with each other. Oswi stood up and spoke " Thane Eldrig, I agree with what you are saying about Farndon and your own troops, however, I sir am I warrior sworn to King Offa as are the troops I command, we will be leaving Farndon to support the King if you wish to support me and provide troops then all the better if you could assist with provisions then we would be grateful, we will be leaving tomorrow morning" with that he stood Bern followed suit and the two men turned and walked from the room.

Thane Eldrig and Lavos shouted insults as they left the hall.

Bern was aware that Oswi would be fuming but had done exceptionally well keeping control of his emotions. They climbed onto their horses and rode out the gate of Farndon to return to Crag Rock.

CHAPTER II
THE SEARCH FOR THE KING

Oswi was fuming as he and Bern rode down the track towards Crag Rock, Bern could see Oswi's hands gripping the reins so tight his knuckles were turning white. Bern had known Oswi many years and he knew it was best to wait he would speak his mind soon enough. The two rode in silence down the track, they soon arrived at Crag Rock the men had finished training for the day and were preparing food for the evening. Bern saw his wife Shia outside their own house she waved a greeting to him. Oswi stopped his horse and jumped down a squire soon ran over to take his animal into the stable. Oswi looked at his old friend and mentor "Could I trouble you to have use of your home for a meeting my friend?" he asked of Bern.

Bern smiled "No problem Oswi I will organise some refreshments who are we involving?"

Oswi stood a moment "You, Ren, Edhert, our squires Ceoal and Raffe too."

"No problem Oswi" replied Bern.

Oswi turned to head to his tent for his map, and then he remembered about the spears. " Bern did Ren and Edhert get those spears organised with Brak do you know"

Bern shook his head " I do not think any got made, why?"

"Well, they could be useful find me Winebert and ask him to go and see Brak, see if he can have some ready for the morning even if we only have enough for the warriors, so that would be twenty, yes twenty ask Brak to sort them if you could" replied Oswi.

Bern nodded and set to the task, shouting for Winebert as he strode out across the yard.

Later that evening Oswi sat with Bern, Ren Edhert, the two squires Ceoal and Raffe had been dismissed to undertake their duties. They had a lot to organise horses, food, fodder and the arms and mail of the warriors.

BERN SAT WATCHING Oswi he could see the young man was troubled by the decisions he had made. Oswi looked up sensing Bern's attention on him "Well we have you, me my father's three warriors and the twelve new trained warriors along with the eight squires as additional support a total of twenty-five men I just hope it will be enough."

Bern smiled "We have a few more Brak will be sending his eldest son also named Brak along and Gava's son Atal, Drax will be coming along with his two hunter friends Acel and Frode all three are great trackers so now we are thirty it is a start to your army" Oswi smiled " Let us hope then it is enough, Bern, let us hope"

Ren and Edhert looked across at Oswi, Ren spoke "Sir the men will not fail you, Bern has tasked us to be the best we may be new to war, but we are ready"

Oswi looked at the two men "Yes you are ready you will be both lead your sections, I will have Bern, Ceoal, Raffe and my father's three warriors and we will have Drax lead Brak, Atal, Acel and Frode as a fourth section the remaining squires can ride in the middle if we need to add weight to a charge then they can circle away and fire their hunting bows to protect our rear".

The sun was only just rising, all the warriors were standing by their horses ready to go, Ceoal and Raffe had worked hard organising the other squires and provisions. Brak had arrived with two mules with the new spears wrapped in bundles, Atal had a mule which had barrels of salted meat strapped to it he ha'd advised Bern it was a gift from Eleen. Bern was clad in his mail his shield with a painted hand holding and an axe was hung on the saddle. Oswi appeared his chain mail dazzled it had been polished so much he wore a dark green cloak around his shoulders matching his own shield of green showing two crossed swords which hung from the saddle of his favourite battled trained horse Alita, a strong dappled grey mare, she gently snorted a welcome as Oswi approached and mounted.

Oswi looked around happy with what he saw he headed out of Crag Rock followed by Bern, Ceoal and Raffe who carried the Kings Pendant and Oswi's gifted from his father the same dark green with crossed swords edged in gold with long golden tassels.

THE JOURNEY STARTED WELL, the troop covered the ground quickly the horses fresh and well-fed fed cantered down the tracks and fields with ease. What surprised Oswi and Bern the most was they found no traces of battle, no birds flocking and feasting on the tender flesh of the dead, no cries or screams of pain from wounded men left after battle, no stray horses, supply carts, abandoned equipment or men who's senses are dulled after battle wondering around. There was not even a smear of blood to be found.

Heading for a trap do you think? Was this planned to get us all out of the way?"

Oswi looked at his friend "I am beginning to think so my friend, we need to be very careful"

The troop reached the old Roman road and began to head inland the gentle thuds as the horses tramped the cobbled road, they soon reached the old stone and wood Roman outpost. This was getting stranger as yet again no sign of battle, and this would have been an ideal bastion for the King to rally his troops at if he had been overwhelmed.

After a brief discussion with Oswi, Bern dispatched his son Drax along with the two hunters Acel and Frode to scout ahead, Bern spoke with Drax "Listen to me son, I do not doubt your skills as a fighter or the hunters, but you must go quietly and carefully, if you find the enemy do not engage them watch them and send a man back to tell us" Drax held his father's gaze " I hear you sir, we will be like wraths in the night, fluttering on the night winds they will neither see or hear our passage, he laughed" Bern shook his head saying "Go" watching them leave Bern laughed himself Drax had the best of both he had his mother Shia's gentle understanding way and ease with anyone but his father's battle skills, and temper when enraged during battle.

The next day Acel and Frode sat across sweat-streaked horses talking with Bern they had found tracks Drax was still moving forward following the tracks, Drax could tell the first set of the smaller party was around a day old but the second was only around four hours old was much larger and obviously following them.

Oswi sent the two hunters back to Drax, and the troop picked up the pace to reach them. As they rode Oswi spoke with Bern " Something is wrong here we were given information from Manse of a battle and the King in trouble, we find neither the King nor signs of a battle." Bern nodded " Also we found tracks which we believe are the Kings and another set showing someone else is following him, either Manse is a seer and knew this was going to happen or we are getting sucked into a plot to kill us and the King" Oswi looked grim-faced at Bern " Not Eldrig or Eleen they have not the guile, Lavos" Bern looked hard at Oswi "Yes my young friend he and that viper Wigson I feel they have set a trap for us with the King as the bait"

Oswi pondered a moment before replying "Ah I think you have

the truth of it, but what puzzles me is the why and who is working with."

They rode on, both rolling the events around in their heads trying to find a solution. A few hours later as night approached and the sky darkened Oswi called a halt and the troop made camp. Bern issued instructions to them all and made sure that nobody would light any fires that evening. Oswi left Bern in charge at the camp he went out searching for the King with Drax, Acel, Frode and young Ceoal. The five of them moved off on foot, they had been walking for some time and Oswi was considering calling a stop, when Frode stopped pointing across the small, wooded valley, they had found them. Oswi crept forward sliding across the dark wet mossy ground so as not to be seen he looked down from the slight rise of his vantage point his heart sank he had found a horde of raiders these must be the ones tracking the King, Oswi sighed and slid back to the men. Oswi looked around Ceoal was not here he heard the familiar owl call over to the right and headed over, Ceoal was hidden from plain view laid across a large dark boulder he was looking into the distance Ceoal had found the King, Oswi slapped the young squire on his back and motioned him to retire to the others.

Oswi sent Ceoal back with Acel and Frode to bring Bern and all the troops forward while he and Drax continued the vigil watching the horde and the King. The chill of the night had Oswi and Drax feeling cold the dark seemed to surround them like a cold, dark blanket, Oswi was sure Bern, and the troops should be nearly here, He heard muffled voices and the chink of armour and weapons, Drax spoke "The raiders are moving lord, they have split into groups and are all on foot I think they plan to encircle the King"

Oswi and Drax moved back down the tracks to try and locate Bern and the troop, if they did not arrive soon, it could be too late to save the King.

. . .

CEOAL, Acel and Frode had made a good time reaching Bern to advise him of the situation. Bern soon had Ren and Edhert organised, and the troop set off with Acel and Frode leading the way the trip was painfully slow the night sky so dark they could not afford to rush and risk injury to man or horse and the troop needed to stay close as not to get lost.

Ceoal spoke to Bern "Sir can we go no faster," "I am concerned about Sir Oswi and Drax," and "What if we are too late" The questions at Bern were endless Bern agreed with Ceoal, but he needed to reach Oswi with a full and intact troop or they would be no use to help the King. Bern just hoped they would be in time and that Oswi had not foolhardily rushed off to try and break through to the King. The night air was chilling but the men and the horses were all sweating with the ride and weight of armour and weapons.

Acel rode back towards Bern "Sir around the next bend then up into the trees is where we left them, Frode has ventured forward on foot as the trees are hard to ride through, I suggest we wait until we find his horse tied up"

Bern let out a huge sigh of relief " Well done Acel, I confess I was beginning to worry, let's move forward as you say and wait for them to come back to us, I hope we are not too late and that Oswi has a plan."

Bern turned to Ceoal and Raffe "Ride the line tell them we will wait round the next bend for Oswi and Drax, advise they eat if they have food on them and drink, I think we are in for a long day, go now boys and return to me"

The two senior squires trotted the line advising the troops when they caught back up with Bern, Oswi stood talking to him.

After a few moments, Oswi called the troop around him, "Men we have a problem the raiders have left to encircle the King we estimate that they outnumber him by around three to one the King is in the bottom of the valley trees are on three sides of him so the raiders will be able to get close, we have not the time to reach and warn the

THE BETRAYAL

King, instead we will wait for the raiders to commit to action and we will counter-attack" The men all nodded in reply as Oswi continued "Listen well men your lives and those of your King and fellow warriors depend on it.

CHAPTER 12
THE KING IS SAVED

Oswi had gone into detail that the troop would make its way down the slope in an arrow formation. He with his section would be the spear point with Drax directly behind him to bulk the head of the charge. Ren would be the left line and Edhert the right they would all charge with the newly designed heavy spears, to punch a gap through the raiders and link with the King, the troop of squires had been tasked to fire arrow after arrow to the sides of the charging troop to deter the raiders but also to hopefully widen the gap and keep firing to keep the gap open. The troops prepared.

The King only knew of the attack with the first clash of weapons and scream of pain. King Offa was in his tent discussing the next area they were to sweep looking for the raiders Ealdorman Ludeca and Alestan sat with him, Ealdorman Sigmund had yet to arrive. A personal guard to the King ran into the tent.

. . .

"My Lord we are under attack, they have broken through the line of sentries, Ealdorman Ludeca's men have formed a shield wall to the North and Ealdorman Alestan's a second line to the South, the enemy look to surround us and Ealdorman Sigmund's men are cut off near the treeline."

King Offa could hear the clamour of battle the clash of axe or sword on shield, the harsh shouted commands of his warriors and the raider scum, the scream of pain from wounded and dying men and the roar of men fighting to stay alive, trapped like rats in a barrel.

King Offa stood "To your men my Lords, the enemy is upon us, hold the lines I will send orders when I have checked how we stand"

The two Ealdorman nodded and ran out into the early morning sky to their hearth-bound warriors.

Ludeca reached his own men quickly, he grabbed a shield from a warrior limping away from the press of bodies massive rents in his chain mail and a deep gash to his shoulder pumping his lifeblood out of him, Ludeca had no time to help him he needed to be in the fight, or all could be lost. Most of his men were engaged shield wall to shield wall with the raider's men pushing shoving grunting with seax sliding below shields to slice open legs and groin, large battle axes swinging over shields to split open skulls like overripe fruit.

Ludeca noticed a pile of spears by the slowly dying fire, he shouted at a few of the young squires.

"You young lads get that fire built up I need flames then find hunting bows and arrows, then wrap lit rags to the arrows and fire over our own troops at the enemy it may slow some of them and ease the pressure on the wall" the young squires grabbed their comrades and jumped to the task all the time the screams and clash of battle tormented their ears and souls. Ludeca had no time for further instructions he pushed between his men ramming his sword down the throat of a raider and was instantly covered in gore and blood, Ludeca let out a roar "OFFA, OFFA," the surrounding men continued the chant as they pushed the raiders back swinging axe, stabbing with sword, and punching the shield into the enemy "Offa, Offa, Offa, Offa."

KING OFFA WAS busy organising the troops across from Ludeca who was to his right, Alestan stood with his own warriors on his left he too was deeply engaged with the raiders. Offa cursed, they had attacked quickly and efficiently the sentries had been killed quietly allowing the mass of raiders to reach the lines of the camp and attack before anybody became aware. King Offa watched as men lay around with faces, arms and legs sliced open the ground was awash with blood. Offa's line of men was spread too thin, so he grabbed a few young men who looked after the horses " Quickly pull those tents down, drag the wounded to lay upon them and then stand ready with my flag" Offa had noticed his standard bearer dead his body half wrapped in his flag, Offa knew they must retreat to the centre of the camp and form a stronger defence of smaller stronger battle lines.

THE INITIAL ATTACK had been swift and deadly Jarl Bjorn had tasked his men to kill and replace the sentries then his men had quickly moved to attack the camp, they had nearly encircled the whole camp when a youth left a tent seeing the raiders he had screamed out a warning to the camp, a few vital minutes lost. Bjorn stood and watched as his men battled pushing and stabbing King Offa's men the wounded soon perished as they were stood on if they fell between the wall of warriors fighting, a few managed to drag themselves clear but he had men quickly end their lives stabbing seax into throats and eyes to finish them. Bjorn looked around he had a number of his own dead and dying but he outnumbered King Offa's men, Bjorn shouted encouragement to his shield warriors "Push them back, swing your axes over their shields weaken the wall we will have them soon."

King Offa stood back from the shield wall and stood with his banner he shouted for his lords "Ludeca, Alestan to me, to me" Alestan heard the shout and stood back from his warriors to step to the King, Ludeca was hard pressed with a huge, black-bearded warrior trying to beat him down with a large double-headed axe, a group of squires jumped forward throwing burning brands at the warrior, whose cloak caught light, and he stepped back from Ludeca to put out the flames. Ludeca slapped the youths on their backs "My thanks lads, nicely done" He too went to his King.

King Offa looked at the two lords both were covered in blood and gore and had rips and dents to their mail. "My Lords, I think we have lost our fight here today, the scum outnumber us and our Ealdorman Sigmund hides watching in the trees" Ludeca spoke first "The men still fight my King" Offa smiled "They do Ludeca and fight proudly we are too few and need to fall to a central ring around the wounded and my standard, we need to push the enemy hard then quickly step back and disengage hopefully a lot of the scum will fall over from the lack of pressure from our warriors so a quick stab to kill or wound as many as we can then they all fall back here to me" Both Lords nodded in agreement Ludeca spoke first my King "We should get the young men to arm themselves it will give strength to them they can dart between our men and stab at the feet and legs of the raider scum"

King Offa smiled " Yes we shall all go down fighting, see to it, my old friend"

. . .

Ludeca and Alestan returned to their hard-pressed warriors more had already fallen one warrior stood pushing his intestines back inside his gut blood gushing down his legs before he collapsed and died. Ludeca saw a young squire his skull smashed open, and his brain split and blood pouring over his face as his body twitched.

Bjorn continued to harass his shield warriors berating them to battle harder, they pushed, kicked, punched, and stabbed at the dwindling wall of King Offa's men. Bjorn was winning he smiled Offa only had a quarter of his men left standing the rest dead or wounded of those who stood in a small circle around the King not one man did not show small wounds or cuts. Bjorn shouted his men back "Hold, men, Hold"

Bjorn stepped forward and shouted for King Offa "Offa, come forward and yield to me, I will have your crown"

Ludeca and Alestan both tried to stop him as he stepped out in front of his men "Scum, you may yet get my crown but only from my dead body, come forward we will cleave more of your warriors to journey on with us"

Bjorn laughed loudly; he had not expected Offa to submit but at least he had balls. He nodded at his men once more "Finish it."

The warriors attacked with renewed vigour, the tall Black bearded warrior attacked where King Offa stood he had three warriors supporting him, and he wanted to be the one to kill Offa.

The fighting was vicious, brutal, and bloody, men hacked off limbs stabbed at eyes and mouths, and sliced at groins all to kill and maim each other, the stench of blood, open guts and men soiling themselves in death was overwhelming. Bjorn's warriors slowly thinned the wall of warriors, Ludeca stood by his King a large cut to his head, and Alestan leaned on a shield he had a gaping wound to his leg, but they would die defending the King.

. . .

NOT THE KING, his warriors or Bjorn and his men felt or heard the slow approach of the thunder of horses. Oswi and Bern led the charging spearpoint attack. Oswi's and the King's banners rippled on the wind as the sun was rising and glinted off the men's armour and shields as they drove the horses at full gallop down the gentle rise of the hill towards the group of raiders surrounding their King. Oswi could see the raiders had encircled the King, this was a desperate charge he hoped it would work, and he manoeuvred his horse so he would hit the largest part of the group of raiders. The squires had peeled away and were now getting their bows and arrows ready to support the action. Oswi signalled to Bern who nodded and raised his arm.

The whole troop levelled the huge spears as they neared the raiders, the spear points gleaming the horses thundered down the last part of the slope the ground shook, and grass and soil flew into the air. Bjorn suddenly felt the ground shake he turned to see the charging horses of mail-clad warriors and the sharp pointed long poled spears, he was momentarily stunned and was unsure what to do, he quickly found his voice "Turn and face the horses" he shouted but such was the clamour and din and roar of men fighting in the shield wall none heard him.

Oswi and his troop quickly closed the gap fast charging horses and men with sharp spears the Banners flapping in the wind, Oswi's heart was pounding he could feel the strength of his horse as she raced to bring him to battle. Oswi was smiling he knew that they could battle through and win the day.

Time seemed to slow as they neared the rear of the raiders, he felt like he could see every detail of action, his troop all charging and screaming, the horses all in mid-stride, the movements of the warriors turning to see them panic on their faces, the King's men shouting in joy. Oswi, Bern and the troop slammed the spears into the raiders the points struck necks, backs, and faces, snatching bodies, and lifting them from the sheer impact, heads brutally split open, spines snapped by the force of the spearhead hitting the body, blood and gore splashed over the thundering horses. Those not killed instantly died under the horses as hoofs smashed open faces, and broke bodies. Oswi steered the troop away from the wall of dying flesh he looked over his shoulder at least thirty raiders were dead and more injured. He shouted instructions to turn the troop for a second charge. Once more the horses charged the noise deafening, the raiders huddled behind battered shields hoping to deflect the horse and spears some broke and ran to be met with a hail of arrows from the squires. The second charge caused more carnage bodies skewered and trampled by horses. Oswi, Bern, Hern, Ludic, and Wulfure all jumped from the back of their horses, Oswi shouted as he could see a large warrior smashing through the King's defence. The King was falling to his knees, and his father and Lord Alestan were also been battered by warriors "TO THE KING" The five men quickly smashed through the raiders, stabbing, and killing as they went Hern and Ludic went to assist Ludeca, Bern pointed at Alestan and Wulfure followed, Oswi rushed to his King who was now on his knees his sword had been smashed from his hand and he was dazed from a blow to the head. The huge, bearded warrior stood poised over him with a grim bloody smile on his recently burnt face and a large gleaming double-headed axe glinting. The King just looked back at him defiantly time slowed as the axe started to fall, the King looked in disbelief as a sword snaked out and sliced across the warrior's throat a bright red spray of blood hit the King and the warrior fell to his knees. Oswi splattered in blood and then slammed his sword into the chest of the warrior who gave a small groan falling dead at the King's feet.

Oswi stood and looked around the raiders had been broken; the few survivors were running from the field. Oswi looked around trying to take it all in.

He knelt by the King "You're safe my lord, they are running away" The King managed a weak smile and a quick reply "Oswi" he then collapsed from his injuries.

CHAPTER 13
THE DEATH

Later that same day Oswi had managed to organise the wounded and those unable to walk or ride were laid on carts. The dead had been piled for a funeral pyre. His father was alive but wounded as was Lord Alestan the King drifted in and out of consciousness, he had managed to thank Oswi and left him in charge.

Ealdorman Sigmund appeared just before evening trying to assert his authority over Oswi. "I am a lord; you will do as I instruct leave the King here and go find a healer and take your men with you they can return to whatever hovel you came from."

Oswi calmly listened to Sigmund before replying " Respectfully Ealdorman Sigmund the King placed me in command therefore I will use your men and horses to assist with transporting the King and his warriors back to Farndon and they will assist me, the King already holds you in a low regard as you hid in the trees and did not aid him"

Sigmund spluttered "You impudent pup, I will" he did not finish as Ealdorman Ludeca and Alestan appeared behind Oswi both were supported by their household warriors Alestan spoke "Sigmund the snake, I see you survived which rock have you crawled out from, our King did place Oswi in charge you would do well to heed what he says"

Sigmund's face was red with anger he had hoped he could force Oswi to relinquish command. "I will not be ordered around by a boy" he turned to his men looking for someone "Ah Harrick, you and your section will stay and assist this, this rabble and the boy leader" Harrick nodded, and Sigmund turned his horse and shouted "Home" to his remaining warriors and galloped away.

HARRICK LOOKED at Oswi "My apologies for my Lord, you will find we are not like him I will set my troop to help with the wounded, I do know that if we head through the woods there is a woodsman and his wife, and she is good at healing"

Oswi smiled "My thanks Harrick, we will set off shortly if you and your section can lead the way"

Harrick nodded "Of course, Sir" he turned to organise his men and help with the wounded.

OSWI TURNED his father and Alestan had returned to sit down he looked at Bern " Well my friend, let us get sorted and head to Farndon we will get Harrick to call on the Woodsman and his good wife to see if she will journey with us to help the King.

It was a slow journey the wounded including the King and Ludeca and Alestan required nearly constant attention. Oswi's troops spent endless hours foraging for food and water, cleaning wounds, and changing bandages. Harrick and his troop had proven themselves; they had located the woodsman Frik and his wife Frey. Frey had bargained with Harrick for a horse and tools for her husband once the price had been agreed she packed up herbs and mosses, bandages and ointments and set to treating the King and his trusted warriors.

HARRICK PLANNED the route back to Farndon with the woodsman Frik who knew paths through the woods which would bring them out north of the old Roman road and that much closer to Farndon.

Oswi checked each morning and evening on the King's condition, Goodwife Frey had cleaned and stitched his wounds she made a poultice to put on his head wound and wrapped it in a clean bandage. The king drifted in and out of consciousness. Oswi's father Ealdorman Ludeca had a deep cut to his shoulder which Goodwife Frey stitched and smeared on a foul-smelling ointment. Ealdorman Ludeca had to confess it may smell bad, but his shoulder was less painful, and the stitched wound gave him little problem. Alestan received similar treatment on his leg and within a few days he could stand with the aid of a crutch.

Some other warriors did not fare as well some succumbed to injuries on the journey their bodies gave out numerous wounds, and Goodwife Frey had to amputate some limbs with help from her husband. Then yet another man whose stomach had been slit open and his intestines were falling out still lived and seemed to be doing well after his treatment of gently pushing everything back in place and stitching him up. Oswi sent Bern, Drax, Acel and Frode on ahead when they were a day from Farndon to request assistance from Thane Eldrig. Bern arrived at Crag Rock and left Drax and the others to sort the settlement and prepare for the warriors to camp and recover here. Drax organised temporary tents to be built to house the men and the wounded would be placed in the long barn. Meanwhile, his father and mother headed to Farndon to speak with Thane Eldrig.

. . .

Slowly after days of care from Goodwife Frey and Shia, Bern's wife the King's condition started to improve. Oswi had pointed out to Eldrig where his duty lay in respect of the King. Oswi had tasked Harrick and his men to guard the King while his own troop was under Ren and Edhert in the recovery of the King's troops. Eldrig was looking frail the events of the past months had left him weak and drained, Eleen was genuinely worried for her father as he had taken to sitting and drinking talking with Lavos who dripped poison into his ear, Eleen spoke with Oswi about this. "I fear my father has given up on his duties, he lets Lavos do more and more every day, and I do not like how he looks at me he has asked my father for my hand in marriage which I said no to" Oswi sat listening "I agree your father seems to have lost the will to fight for Farndon and Lavos seems to be taking control, there is little I can do. I cannot take control of Farndon from your father; we need the King to recover" Eleen smiled weakly, and both sat watching the night sky.

The days rolled on the King slowly looking healthier each day, and Eldrig looking worse each day, Lavos was strutting around like he was the Lord of Farndon. Rolf the steward of Farndon had also complained at Oswi that Lavos was taking coins from the treasury. Oswi supported Eleen where he could and tried his best to counterbalance the negative impact Lavos and his gang were having. Oswi noticed that those warriors loyal to Lavos all sported new clothing and chainmail they even had new swords and seaxes. Oswi decided that in the morning he would go and speak with Eldrig, he hoped the old man would listen to him and dispose of Lavos before it was too late.

Oswi called the next morning at Crag Rock to check on his own and the King's troops, they along with his fathers and Ealdorman Alestan were recovering well a few more had passed away from wounds. Oswi himself had lost five warriors and three squires in the battle to reach the King, he would need to search for new recruits once the

King was fully recovered. Oswi had started once more with the plans to improve the defences at Farndon which had been part of his remit from the King. Oswi was walking back up the track from Crag Rock to Farndon when he saw Bern at full gallop heading out of the gate with Oswi's own horse on a lead following, it took no time for Bern to reach him. Oswi grabbed his horse and jumped into the saddle "Is it the King" he enquired, Bern looked at him "No my friend it's worse, Eldrig is dead and Lavos is trying to take control and evict the king and his men from Farndon" Oswi grimaced "Right back to Farndon get Harrick and half of his troop and we will go to the hall, I take it that is where Lavos and his supporters are?" Bern nodded "Yes should I ask your father and Lord Alestan to attend?" "Yes, do that but suggest they remain behind the men and only speak if needed."

Oswi arrived at the hall to find Aruth, Ceolstan, Thrun, and Wareson along with Brak and Gava, Aruth spoke first "We will go with you, Lavos is making out he is the new Thane he has locked Eleen away and said she is his bride to be"

Oswi shook his head "Right let's go keep your hands off your swords, I am going to demand he steps down and I will assume command in the King's name until he can appoint a new Thane and that he release Eleen to me as the King's commander." The group all smiled, Oswi had their support and Harrick and his troops and his own command.

Oswi decided he needed to be forceful Harrick arrived with Bern along with Ludeca and Alestan, it was then that Oswi decided to make his move he threw open the double doors to the hall the sunlight streamed in behind him and he marched down the central aisle quickly taking in the scene Lavos was sat in the Thane's chair at the table with his warriors Wigson, Lud, Beorn, Cernwulf, Thornhed and a few others who knew no better, Rolf the steward was arguing loudly with Lavos about he could not take control. It was at this point that Oswi marched along shouting as he walked the loyal troops of Eldrig, along with Harrick's warriors fanned out behind him.

"Lavos, you will stop this charade now, you have no legal right to assume command or lordship over this village or claim the hand of the Thane's daughter Eleen whom you hold captive and will release her to my custody and care, I am the appointed commander of King Offa's army here in this region and by want of law I speak with the King's authority and power as if I where the King, you will yield to me on this matter NOW. The steward Rolf can take on the mantle of governorship of Farndon until the King can take appropriate action, DO NOT FORCE ME TO TAKE ANY OTHER ACTION." Oswi had now arrived on the raised platform and stood directly in front of Lavos his hands rested on his sword and seax. Lavos stood pushing the chair over his hand went to his own sword Oswi was faster and before Lavos had half pulled his sword out Oswi's was nestled against his throat. "DO NOT" Oswi said firmly. Lavos released the hilt and his face set like stone Wigson, and the others all stepped away from Lavos and Oswi, "You men here disperse to your duties" snapped Oswi, "Rolf remove the keys from Captain Lavos and release Eleen" "Yes my Lord" Rolf replied keen to be away from the situation. Oswi turned "Aruth go with the steward and escort Eleen here she will stay with my father and Ealdorman Alestan they can be her appointed guardians" Aruth nodded and set off after Rolf. Oswi was pleased with how quickly he had controlled the situation he spoke once more "Harrick could you allocate four men to escort Lavos from here and make sure he remains within the confines of his dwelling" Harrick pointed at four men who strode forward grabbing Lavos and marching him form the hall.

The other warriors of Harrick's dispersed to their duties leaving Oswi, his father, Bern, and Ealdorman Alestan in the hall.

Ealdorman Alestan clapped Oswi on the back laughing "Well you showed him young Oswi remind me not to piss you off"

Eleen appeared and ran straight to the arms of Oswi, sobbing in her relief of freedom and grief for her father.

"Eleen, calm yourself my father and Ealdorman Alestan will act as your guardians, Lavos is confined to his quarters with a guard, and I have given Farndon to Rolf to manage in the absence of a Thane. We will see what the King has to say of the events when he is recovered."

Eleen managed a weak smile "Thank you Oswi, will you assist me with arranging for my father's burial" Oswi smiled down at Eleen "Of course, go now with my father and take Ethane with you to assist and be your companion we will send Goodwife Frey and Shia to see you they may have something to help calm you after the day you have had."

Eleen nodded and took the arm of Ealdorman Ludeca and left the hall, Ealdorman Alestan winked at Oswi "That girl is in love with you young Oswi" he smiled and followed Ludeca and Eleen out of the hall. Oswi sagged "This village is tasking me" Bern just burst out laughing at Oswi.

CHAPTER 14
THE HONOUR

Oswi did not see much of Eleen over the next few days. He would have liked to as he had deep feelings for her, he had assisted with the funeral of her late father Thane Eldrig. The whole village had turned out for his burial he was placed alongside his father and grandfather the previous Thane of Farndon. Rolf the steward of Farndon had arranged a feast for the whole village which was held out in the open courtyard, Gava had roasted some boars and swans which had been caught recently and the village women cooked up fresh breads and fish to complete the feast. Ealdorman Ludeca and Alestan arranged for barrels of ale to be supplied from their own purse. Eleen had not eaten much or spoken during the funeral and feast but did acknowledge and thank everyone.

Oswi was kept busy meeting with Rolf and the village elders and planning the defence improvements with Aruth and Bern. Checking with Goodwife Frey and Shia and the King's welfare and the remaining troops still wounded. Liaising with Ren and Edhert regards the training of his troop, Ceoal Oswi's squire was kept busy from sun up to sun down running errands and taking messages to different people. Oswi was lucky in his squire as like Oswi Ceoal was the youngest son of a Lord and had been well educated he could read and write and had taken instruction in warfare from an early age, Oswi knew he needed to speak with the King and request that Ceoal be assigned as a warrior to his troop, he had earned it.

THE KING CONTINUED to improve and was now sat up talking with Bern and Ealdorman Ludeca and Alestan. Oswi had not visited the King himself he was too busy. Lavos continued to be held at his dwelling he was allowed no visitors and had a constant pair of guards stationed to watch him Harrick organised this and the arrangement of feeding Lavos, at least Oswi did not have that to deal with. Harrick unlike his Ealdorman Sigmund had proved a valuable asset to Oswi. Harrick was an excellent organiser and liked by his section of men who worked hard, Oswi needed to speak with the King about Harrick too he needed a different position away from Sigmund maybe assigned to the King permanently.

OSWI HAD JUST ARRIVED BACK at Farndon after a meeting out in the lower wood where he had been discussing which trees to use to improve the defences with the woodsman Frik, he had proved very knowledgeable about the type of trees to use, and which trees were in good health to chop down he advised how to cut and prepare the trees for the different parts of the new wall and gate. Oswi had kept both Frik and his wife Frey longer than the agreement with Harrick and he knew that he owed Frik more in compensation.

Ceoal was standing waiting at the gate of Farndon when Oswi arrived "Sir you need to quickly freshen yourself up, come quickly here to the stables I have some water and a fresh shirt for you, we need to make you look presentable"

Oswi looked down from his horse at Ceoal, "What is the panic now

young Ceoal, Does the King demand my presence?" he laughed.

Ceoal looked at Oswi and smiled "Yes he does, he has been waiting for you in Thane Eldrig's Hall"

Oswi gulped "Quickly then let us get about this" he said jumping down and running to the stable.

Ceoal walked alongside Oswi as they both approached the hall, Aruth was stood waiting outside. "Oswi, the king is inside along with your father and Alestan other Lords arrived including Sigmund who may yet be removed as a Lord and expelled from Mercia" Oswi smiled "Well the turd deserves that, he showed cowardice in front of his King not a good idea" "Yes" replied Aruth who continued "The King has been informed by Eleen of the events leading up to your timely rescue of the King, and the events leading to the death of our Thane and the holding of captain Lavos, who is also inside the hall, Bern, myself, Brak, Gava and Rolf have all been called and verified the events that Eleen has spoken of, now he awaits you." Oswi gulped hard "Oh great, will I manage to leave here with my head still attached" he smiled at Aruth. "Come open the doors and allow me entrance to my King.

Oswi was startled as Aruth took hold of the ornate handle of the door and swung it hard, so it knocked against the old oak doors the sound seemed to thunder in Oswi's ears.

THE DOORS slowly opened inwards pulled open by two of Harrick's warriors. The light shone brightly behind Oswi casting his shadow and that of Aruth and Ceoal down the middle of the hall.

Aruth spoke "Walk forward to the King sir" Oswi startled began to walk down the central aisle of the hall which he noticed was filled with warriors, villagers, and Lords, Rolf, Eleen, his own troop with

THE BETRAYAL

Ren and Edhert, his father was stood smiling next to King Offa, Oswi noticed Lavos stood under guard to one side with Harrick nearby, that made Oswi smile. The King stood and beckoned Oswi "Come forward Oswi"

He stepped out down the hall with Ceoal two steps behind him and stopped before the raised platform where King Offa and his father stood.

The King looked at Oswi and smiled "Your late Oswi, not good to keep your King waiting"

Oswi bowed "My apologises Lord King I was busy with the woodsman picking trees for the new village gate and did not know my presence was required"

King Offa laughed " I hope you picked good strong trees, now to the task in hand. Our Lady Eleen has provided me with the background to how you and your troop ended up arriving at the right moment to save me from certain death. The steward has explained the quick decline in the health of our recently departed Thane Eldrig. I have seen first-hand the plans you have to reinforce the village and the work you have done to re-establish Crag Rock. I have also seen first-hand the commitment and calibre of the troops Bern and you trained."

Oswi bowed again "Thank you, Lord King"

King Offa continued, "I am therefore fully aware of the events while I have been in recovery " Oswi politely nodded his head as the King continued "I have spoken with many people about the issues and problems you have dealt with during my time of absence. I do not need any information from you as yet, I have one item we will discuss shortly" The King at this point looked at Lavos, before continuing "What I require from you Oswi at this time is the names of any man who has assisted you and you feel is deserving of a reward from his King"

Oswi was momentarily stunned he had expected to have to discuss all his actions these past weeks, but he realised the King was very well informed, Oswi looked at King Offa "Thank you Lord King yes I have some people deserving of a reward, Firstly Rolf steward of Farndon he deserves recognition" The King nodded and turned to a scribe "Note Rolf's name, we will provide him with a reward of money to help him live comfortable in his later life, continue Oswi"

Oswi looked at Harrick "Harrick, my King a senior warrior of Lord Sigmund may I request he take my place as a captain in your guard and train your new warriors" Harrick was stunned by the request Oswi had made his body hummed with the thrill of the proposal "Agreed, next" said King Offa.

Oswi went on Brak the smith to be commissioned to the King to train new smiths in weaponry, Ren and Edhert to be appointed their troop of warriors under the King, the woodsman and his Goodwife to be built a new home at Crag Rock, the list went on each time the King agreed Oswi wanted to promote Aruth but felt that should be for the new Thane of Farndon to look at but he would try and assist with that, at no time did Oswi even contemplate asking for a reward for his services in saving the King. Oswi looked at the King "I have a final request Lord King" Oswi stepped to one side and waved Ceoal his squire forward "This my Lord King is Ceoal fifth son of Ealdorman Cernwulf in the north of Mercia, he has acted as my squire for some time and showed great bravery and skill during our recent adventures, I would like to request he is allowed to be appointed as a warrior in my troop" The King looked at Ceoal "Step forward" Ceoal did do though very nervously "Ceoal, we will do as Oswi requests I hear you stayed close to Oswi during the action flying my banner, I, therefore, will supply you with a new sword and chainmail as a warrior under Oswi" Ceoal was stunned and managed to stammer a reply "Thhh thank you Lord King" the King laughed and looked at Oswi, "Come to Oswi stand here at my side"

Oswi stepped up and stood by the side of his King he looked around the hall which was full of people he knew, who had lived, breathed, and fought alongside.

Oswi suddenly realised that the king was speaking to the assembled Lords, and he had heard his own name mentioned: "What do

THE BETRAYAL

you say you my Lords I require an agreement from you all, here stands a loyal warrior of your King, will you consent to his appointment as the new Thane of Farndon and Crag Rock to maintain the area and improve it, to raise troops for his King and guard the river from raiders, he will also provide shelter for our Lady Eleen with the absence of her father until we can provide a suitable marriage for her, do you all agree?"

Oswi could not believe his ears, he was stunned and lost, and looking around he saw the assembled Lords his father, Alestan and others he knew by face rather than name, he could see Bern shouting and Eleen clapping her hands he looked around the hall the faces of these he knew blurring as he scanned around, he became aware of the shouting and agreeing of the Lords as each answered in turn his father the last to voice "I agree" Oswi looked upon his father's smiling face, grinning back, Oswi the youngest of his father Ealdorman Ludeca had never expected he would get a title and land to call his own, he had planned to live his life following the King and training his troops.

The King stepped forward clasping Oswi's forearm Oswi, "Oswi, son of Ealdorman Ludeca, we appoint you as Thane of Farndon and Crag Rock, you will rule here by my appointment and establish training for more troops, we will leave you Bern and Ceoal and a section of men from your original troop, the rest of the warriors will return with me to Repton where Harrick will take on your mantel of captain and trainer." It was then that Lavos started "You would appoint him as Thane I was promised it by Eldrig, Farndon is mine" The King stepped quickly down from the platform walked quickly up to Lavos and punched him hard in the face "Still your voice cretin, you had no rights to Farndon you are scum to me, you are not even fit to hold the rank of captain of the guard, you will be left here to take on sentry duties and be happy I do not insult you further, you may leave the service of Thane Oswi if you have somewhere to go" without waiting for an answer King Offa returned to "Oswi come we will talk with the Lords as I will be leaving tomorrow"

The hall dispersed Lavos was left alone and stood seething, his face a mask of anger what could he do now he had demanded much of Jarl Bjorn and provided nothing in return he was supposed to provide a sanctuary for Bjorn's fleet, Bjorn would already be angry after the failed killing of Offa, Lavos needed to plan again.

CHAPTER 15
THE KIDNAP

The next morning Oswi was standing in the courtyard saying his farewells to Ren, Edhert who would command their troops of warriors for the King. Harrick came next he was truly humbled with his new position, he thanked Oswi and called a young man forward "Thane Oswi this is Vern my second son he has recently arrived from our home, I would ask you if I could" Oswi looked at Harrick "Ask away my friend if I can assist you I will" Harrick took a deep breath "I feel my new role could be tasking and dangerous I would ask that you take my son on as your new squire as you require a replacement for Ceoal" Oswi looked at Ceoal stood nearby who had heard the conversation, he knew Harrick asked much of Oswi as the position of the squire was usually reserved for younger sons of other Lords, Ceoal stepped forward and looked at Vern "Tell me how would you get rust from your Lords chainmail" Vern smiled easy sir with sand and vinegar " Ceoal turned to Oswi and simply nodded. Oswi smiled "I will take the lad from you Harrick but he needs to know Ceoal will work him hard from dawn till dusk in his duties as a squire we will also train him in weapons," Oswi looked at Vern "Can you read or write he asked" Vern blushed

"My mother tried to teach me but I was erm difficult my Lord" Oswi looked hard at him "Vern to be a good squire you need to relay my messages and therefore to remain my squire you will learn I will request a daily session with Lady Eleen to school you are we agreed?" Vern to his credit did not hesitate or look to his father "I do my Lord" Oswi nodded and clasped arms with Harrick "I will treat him well my friend and you are always welcome at my hearth" "Thank you Oswi" With that he turned and moved away.

EALDORMAN LUDECA CAME to speak with his son "Oswi know I am proud of you I was honoured when you were chosen to captain the King's guard, but the reward you have now and the land you own well it is truly wonderful your mother will be proud too, take care I will see you soon"

Oswi climbed up to stand on the wall as he watched the King, Lords and warriors leave, the King had left him a final gift a bag of gold to use as he saw fit. Bern and Ceoal stood on each side of Oswi as they watched the group disappear from view Oswi turned and looked down into the courtyard. He had a troop of twelve warriors who would be commanded by Bern and Ceoal. The original warriors of Farndon stood next to them in three groups, the first consisted of Lavos, Wigson, Lud, Beorn, Cernwulf, and Thornhed all hard faced, the second group Aruth, Hardison, Loff, Ceolstan, Thrun, Wareson to one side stood the third group Drax, Brak the younger, Atal, Acel, Frode and Wulfure a warrior of his fathers who had requested to stay behind as he now had a limp from the battle to save the King.

OSWI COULD SEE across the courtyard where Rolf stood with Eleen and her maid Ethane. Oswi needed to address the troops and warriors.

"Men I am pleased you are all here to help me protect Farndon and Crag Rock, we must work together to make Farndon strong against the raiders, any man who feels he does not wish to remain under my command must say now, I will provide any man a horse, food and weapons should he wish to leave" Oswi waited he had hoped Lavos and the others would take the hint but none spoke or moved, Oswi spoke again "Thank you, any past issues will be put aside we need to work together, Bern and Ceoal will command the troop of King's men who remain here, we will now decide who will captain the guard of Farndon, would any man like to be considered?" again Oswi said this to see if Lavos had prepared any of his men to step forward none did. The silence was broken by Wulfure "My Lord, I stay with you as I now carry a limp I am no good to you to lead but I would like to put Aruth forward as captain" Oswi smiled "My thanks Wulfure" Suddenly Thrun, Wareson, Drax, Brak, Atal and others all shouted in agreement. Then a soft feminine voice spoke through the harsh noise of the men "My Lord Oswi I would also like to nominate Aruth he is a loyal, honest and trustworthy man, he will not let you down and would willing to lay down his life for you and Farndon" Oswi smiled at Eleen and bowed his head he looked down at the men stood before him he had wanted Aruth but was happy the men had also chosen him he spoke once more "It is agreed from this day Aruth will be your captain and wear a bronze arm ring as a sign of his rank, thank you all please be about your duties Aruth, Bern, Ceoal and Rolf would you join me in the hall"

Oswi and the others went into the hall. Oswi had arranged a large table with benches to be placed on the raised platform. The servants had already placed a large dish of pottage, bread, and drink on the table. Oswi sat at the head "Sit my friends sit" The others all sat down young Vern followed too and Ceoal motioned for him to sit at the far end of the table. Oswi spoke "I have decided to make some changes to how we manage Farndon, I may well be the Thane, but I confess I do not know everything, we will have breakfast each morning as a group to discuss what we need to do and prioritise our work" Oswi looked around the group. "Rolf as a steward you will deal with the general running of Farndon including the trade and commerce side of things, we will look to find someone to assist you with your duties on the trade element" Rolf smiled "Thank you, my Lord, that would be helpful, a fresh mind would assist me greatly on the trade side" Oswi smiled "Think of someone who could assist they need to be good with figures and be able to read and write, then we will speak with them together, Aruth you will manage the security of the village wall and the old watchtower, you have three groups of men currently I wish for a fourth group to be created, Wulfure will be a leader of his section, Wareson can take over your section but you will need a replacement also. We will leave Lavos to lead his section for now, so we need in total a section leader and six men" Aruth replied "If I could request a few days away from Farndon and take Wulfure, Ceoal and Raffe with me, Harrick mentioned that some of the former warriors of Lord Sigmund are seeking a new Lord we could try those first." Oswi nodded in agreement "Yes a good idea but bring back more than we require and we can then pick the best of them, Bern you and the troop will still be based at Crag Rock, you will also be in charge of making sure Brak and the new smiths make weapons for us to stockpile for the King" Bern laughed "Have no fear with Brak he has plans in place and has recruited a smith from Lord Sigmund's employ and three new boys to train, he will meet the Kings demands" Oswi knew Brak would not let the King down "Good news, lastly Ceoal once you return with Aruth you will manage the teams of men and women building the new gatehouse and wall, you will also meet regularly with woodsman Frik to learn about the different trees and the best materials to use, he is very knowledgeable" Ceoal nodded "Yes my lord, could I bring Raffe in with me he is hard working and has some additional ideas to strengthen the wall" "Yes of course" Replied Oswi.

"Well then let us have breakfast and be about our duties, Oh one more item, I have agreed that Lady Eleen and her maid Ethane can remain here in their original quarters in the hall, I will also take up residence here in the former quarters of Eldrig, Lady Eleen will be allowed every courtesy of her rank she is of Farndon and will not be seen as a guest, I will be requesting that she assist and learn my new squire and some of the other younger ones in reading and writing to benefit us all, I know Ceoal, Rolf and myself are able if any other wishes to benefit from the lesson let me know" Aruth smiled "I would wish to learn my Lord, I feel it would benefit my role and advancement" "Agreed Aruth" replied Oswi. Bern stayed quiet he had never learned and had no interest at his age he had made sure his sons could, but he was content he knew Oswi would not push him. The group set about devouring the food before they left to pursue their duties.

The village was busy, Oswi was constantly called upon to check food stocks, meet with merchants and visitors, check the troops and the work on the gate and wall, and agree on monies to be spent, he felt drained each day, he hoped he would get used to it. His new squire Vern was doing well he prepared fresh hot water and food each morning for Oswi ran errands during the day and before the last meal he sat for a time with Lady Eleen to receive his lessons. Bern was kept busy with his dealings with Brak. Rolf had managed to negotiate a deal with a new merchant requiring a safe place to keep his boat and would pay for the privilege but also supply goods at a discounted rate to Farndon.

Aruth and the others returned to Farndon around a week later, with a group of warriors and a few other people he had left them all in the courtyard and sought out Oswi who was busy with Rolf discussing increasing the size of the food winter storage shed. "Aruth good to see you is all well?" Oswi asked as he noticed Aruth stride through the door. "Yes my lord it is I have brought ten men who would like to be considered to join as guards, the senior man named Drom a huge bear of a man is an old companion to Harrick, I have also brought a family who wish to set up here as bakers of bread to supply you and Farndon, we also have a few others who are experienced with crops and animals so I wonder if they could help Bern at Crag Rock" Replied Aruth. "Bring the baker and his family first to the hall I will speak with them, then the workers, Bern is about with Brak so ask him to join me, then Bern, Ceoal, you, and I will assess the warriors and see if we can use them." Replied Oswi, he and Rolf returned to the hall as Aruth set to his tasks.

Oswi was pleased with the arrival of Lorik and his family and agreed they could stay, and he would provide a building they could work from to supply bread, he left Rolf to deal with that. The three male workers spoke with Oswi, and Bern one had a young family the others were two single men, but their hands were deeply marked and grimy showing they would work hard, they were all sent down the road to Crag Rock they would live and work the land around it.

Oswi went outside to the courtyard to find Aruth stood with the ten warriors. Bern spoke as they walked over to them "Well we can tell who Drom is look at the size of him it is like a walking talking bear"

Oswi giggled "You can go tickle his belly and see if he growls, let us put them through their paces and see if we can get enough men Drom looks capable as the section leader so we require six other warriors" Aruth along with Bern set the men through a set of challenges first they did sword and shield work, then axes, archery followed. Oswi then sent them for a run before a final bout of what could only be described as a fist fight. Drom was the only man still standing at the end. Oswi chatted with Bern and Aruth and they decided on the six men that they required, the unlucky ones Oswi spoke "Men you were unlucky today, but I have my quota of new men, I will provide you all with food, drink, and a roof for the night and in the morning a coin each before you leave." Only one spoke a skinny older man who had done well until the running "Thank you, Lord"

Oswi left Aruth to organise the new warriors, feeding and sheltering them.

THE BETRAYAL

. . .

OSWI WAS JUST ABOUT to get out of bed the next morning the sun was still yet to rise when Vern came running, smashing the door open and breathlessly stumbling on his words "My, My Lord, Aruth requires you at the gate Wulfure, he, he is dead my Lord and I have been told to say the gate is open too." Oswi was stunned he dressed quickly grabbing his sword as he ran from the room down the hall and out into the courtyard where warriors stood around waiting.

Earlier that night Eleen had been in bed something had woken her a small bump and a scuffle, Ethane climbed from her bed grabbed a heavy woollen cloak, and wrapped it around her shoulders, she made for the small door that joined hers with Ethane's grabbing the metal handle pulled the door open she stepped inside the dark room she was already across the threshold when she felt the presence of another she turned to see Wigson on her right she was about to scream when a huge hand fastened about her mouth her eyes were wide in fear she could feel a chill down her spine the huge maul of a hand turned her face and she looked up into the insane grin of Lavos, her knees went weak and she half fell to the floor. Lavos spoke "Bind her hands and gag her I'll grab some clothes for her then we head to the gate" Wigson and Lud both nodded and set about the task.

Once they were sorted Lavos threw Eleen across his shoulder, and they quickly left the rooms and went out of a side door of the hall into the courtyard area.

LUD STEPPED OUT FIRST and bumped into a man, both tumbled to the ground Lud jumped up first and drew his seax, the man he had fallen over was the skinny warrior who had failed to meet Thane Oswi's grade as a warrior. He stood looking at the scene unfolding before him, he spoke first "Hello my friends do you have Thane's permission to be stealing young ladies in the dead of night?" he had seen

Lud draw a blade, he had two small blades tucked in his belt behind his back and his seax still in its sheath.

Wigson spoke to Lud "Kill him" Wigson and Lavos both turned to step away, and as Lud stepped forward to end the man's life, the man stepped to his left drawing a blade from his back and stabbing Lud in his eye Lud was dead before he hit the ground the man grabbed Lud's seax and stepped forward, Wigson turned sword in hand Lavos grunted and dropped Eleen to the floor who screamed as the hard floor jolted her. Both stepped towards the skinny man, he jumped forward slashing the seax across the nose of Wigson momentarily blinding him, he drew his second small blade and slammed it into the thigh of Lavos, who grimaced in pain, the fight ended as Wigson recovered and slammed his seax into the side of the warrior as Lavos slammed a fist into his head the skinny warrior fell to the floor. Lavos quickly grabbed Eleen again who was trying to crawl away she had seen the bravery of the skinny warrior and hoped he lived.

Lavos and Wigson went to the main gate and met Beorn, Cernwulf, and Thornhed. Lavos spoke as two other warriors approached from the steps to the rampart above the gate "All good" the two men nodded "Yes the man on duty will not hear us leave" Lavos smiled these two others had tried for positions as guards, but Wigson had recognised them from his days trading and knew they were scum, so Lavos quickly recruited them. Beorn spoke, "Hey where is Lud?" Wigson replied "Dead, now let us get away before anyone else sees us" The group left through the gate the horse's hoofs had rags wrapped about them so they made less noise, Lavos hoped they could be well away from Farndon before dawn. Early in the night Lavos and his men had been on duty, he had sent men out with horses to wander the paths and cause confusion to any tracks they would make.

CHAPTER 16
THE RESCUE

Oswi, Bern, Aruth, and Ceoal stood looking down on Wulfure. Oswi was upset he had known Wulfure all his life, he had been a warrior of his father. He looked at the others "Call all the men in we need to see if anyone else is missing" Bern nodded and turned to obey as he did he saw a warrior stumbling from the rear of the hall the man looked up and drew breath trying to shout "My lord" was all he could say before falling once more to the ground. Bern was the first to the man's side, rolling him over he noticed the blood-drenched tunic and wound "he is wounded Oswi" Oswi knelt at his side and looked up for Ceoal "Find me, Goodwife Frey, NOW" Ceoal dashed off as the man grabbed the tunic of Oswi "I tried to stop him, killed one back there," Aruth ran off to check he found Lud and came back whispering to Oswi "Lud, blade in his eye" Oswi nodded and looked back to the bleeding warrior who spoke again "It was the big man La, Lavos, he took your lady, I tried" the man fainted at this point, Goodwife Frey arrived pushing the men aside she requested he be moved and warriors came and lifted him.

. . .

OSWI STEPPED BACK LOOKING at Aruth and Bern he set off at a run to Eleen's quarters, panic etched over his face. Oswi burst into Eleen's room she was gone Aruth opened Ethane's to find her tied and gagged on her bed. Aruth freed her sobbing Ethane spoke of the night, "Lavos, Wigson, and Lud, they grabbed me and tied me up they wanted Lady Eleen, I heard them talking that the others were outside getting the horses while their two new friends would open the gate." Poor Ethane sobbed her way through the tale as Oswi, Bern, and Aruth listened. Bern spoke first come Ethane let us get Shia to look at those wrists and the lump on your head. He took her out of the room as Ceoal turned up.

Thane Oswi "The man Lan is settled Goodwife Frey says he should recover, it is a clean cut, and he was knocked out."

Oswi looked up "Who is he?" Aruth answered "He was one of the men who did not obtain a position with you" Oswi looked at Aruth "Well he has one now he deserves that, did he say more Ceoal" Ceoal replied "Yes he told me how he knifed Lud through the eye and smashed a blade across Wigson's face, and stabbed Lavos in the thigh, a brave man taking on three warriors" Oswi sighed "Yes and not even of Farndon, so we have Lavos and his gang running with Eleen as a captive, Ceoal find Bern and assemble the King's troop, Aruth you and your men will stay here and defend Farndon just in case." The two nodded and went about their duties.

OSWI LEFT and walked across to speak with the man Lan, he owed him his thanks for trying to assist Eleen, he could have lost his life.

Oswi was annoyed he had hoped Lavos would get on with his duties he obviously wanted Farndon as his own along with Eleen and Oswi now wondered if the events of the attacks and Crag Rock the attack on the King had been designed by Lavos. Oswi soon reached the stable to find Lan laid out on his side clean and wrapped in bandages and a compress on the lump on his head, Goodwife Frey nodded at him "He will live I have stitched the wounds and applied a poultice to keep infection away, he needs rest now" Oswi smiled "Thank you, I am glad you stayed around" Frey spoke once more, "Frik has already gone out to try and track which way they have gone, that poor sweet thing taken by them" Oswi had not known Frik had left but he would find the tracks and hopefully they could catch them up. "I will have a quick chat with Lan before I leave to chase them down" Oswi turned and knelt next to Lan "Lan I would like to thank you for your efforts, you took down one man and wounded the other two, by good fortune they did not kill you and we now know who took Lady Eleen, you will stay here in the care of Goodwife Frey and when I return I will appoint you to my guard here at Farndon, I would like you to take over from Wulfure as section leader who was killed last night, would this be acceptable to you?"

Lan smiled "It would and thank you I may be getting older, but I have proved I can still fight, I will be your man" Oswi smiled and grabbed the forearm that Lan had outstretched to him. He stood and left to find Bern they needed to be away.

On entering the courtyard, he found Bern and Aruth waiting for the King's troop assembled and his horse and armour ready. Aruth grabbed Oswi's chainmail to help him, "Come let us get you sorted, Ceoal left with Frik to find tracks and should be heading back soon while Frik continues with the trail" "That is great" replied Oswi as the mail was pulled over his head. Oswi was ready and took his place at the front of the troop next to Bern, Oswi gave a slight nod and Bern spoke "Troop advance" They headed out the gate and down the slope of the path onto the track Oswi looked around and spotted Ceoal across the river he addressed the troop "Troop turn right advance to the bridge" Bern and Oswi galloped in front and met Ceoal at the far side.

"Crafty buggers they were they laid false tracks heading inland, Frik soon realised, and we headed back and across the river, the tracks skirt the hill and village of Holt and head down the river towards Wrexham, Frik is still on the trail, but he is leaving markers as he goes" reported Ceoal, Oswi looked around seeing the hill and village of Holt and the river twisting away open fields surrounded the area and tracks led away into the distance. "Come let us catch Frik we will move at a trot we need to catch them before Wrexham if that is their goal, last I heard the Raiders now held it, we will fail if they reach Wrexham" With that they set off covering ground quickly Ceoal led with another warrior searching for the signs a cross on a tree or twisted plant to show the way.

THE TROOP soon covered some distance Bern had advised caution as they moved deeper into Powys towards Wrexham. The day moved on, Oswi kept the troop moving they ate and drank in the saddle but had still not caught up with Frik or Lavos and his gang. Oswi was getting worried that Frik was on the wrong trail what would he say to the King if he lost Eleen, Oswi was supposed to protect her. The sun slowly began to set and Oswi slowed the troop to a walk a small huddle of rocks could be seen in the distance and Ceoal reported Frik was waiting at them. A short time later Oswi, Bern, and Frik were stood away from the men talking, Frik pointed to a wood and a hill a distance in front, "That is where they are in a small cave on the other side of the hill, I have checked in front and believe they could reach Wrexham probably late tomorrow, during the night at the latest." Bern looked and Oswi who looked momentarily defeated, he turned to Frik " Could you lead a section of men around so they could come to the cave form the other side?" Frik looked at the sky they would need to go now before dark and then camp with no fires to be in place, but I can do it." Bern looked to Oswi "You wish to split the troop and attack from two sides Oswi" queried Bern "Yes that is my plan I will take Ceoal and three others along with Frik we will head out now while we still have enough light to see and wait in the woods beyond the cave, you and the rest of the troop can camp here and move forward before dawn, when you get close to the camp you can let them hear you hopefully they will panic and head straight out of the wood to where we wait they should be spread out and looking to escape and we should be able to attack and release Eleen" Bern scratched his chin as he always did when pondering an outcome, "It could work but you risk much traveling in near dark as we will moving forward before dawn, but I can think of no other plan so let us be about it we will rest now, you must leave with Frik" Bern spoke quickly calling Ceoal and three good strong fighting warriors forward he spoke briefly to them "You all leave with Lord Oswi, he has a plan he will explain on the way, go quickly and quietly with him but DO NOT return without him" The warriors all looked at Bern and nodded their understanding. Bern told the rest of the troop to rest, eat, drink sleep, and post a guard as the men did as he instructed he stood watching Oswi and the others head over to the fields soon to be swallowed by the darkness of the night as it crept in like some dark consuming shadow.

FRIK WAS good he trotted his small pony over the fields and round through a shallow river bed, which led to the other side of the wood Oswi could hardly see his horse's head let alone the route to take they all followed close to each other a few times during the trip a horse would stumble Ceoal even fell from his horse causing the rest to laugh at his misfortune. It was pitch black by the time the small group reached the edge of the forest, Oswi told everyone to get some rest both he and Frik pushed through the long grass and trees to watch he could make out the shapes of the men, and counted seven men, Frik pointed and spoke in a whisper "She is there sat by the entrance" Oswi looked hard then as the moon shone through a gap in the clouds he saw her Eleen sat on a log, hands tied, but alive. He let out a slow breath and he and Frik slipped away back to the resting men. Oswi hoped the plan would work he was gambling that Lavos would not wish to be caught and they could grab Eleen his only risk with the plan was that Lavos would kill Eleen at the first sign of trouble.

Bern struggled to rest he was worried about Oswi and how this would end he hoped at least Oswi, and Eleen would be safe when tomorrow was over, Bern did eventually fall asleep and was shaken awake by one of the troopers as the first rays of sun flickered across the trees and fields. Bern looked at the troop horses stood ready including his own, he quickly rolled up his cloak and nodded at his men "Well done all, come we will go and wake Lavos and his companions up, remember the idea is to startle them and drive them out of the trees into the fields beyond where the others are waiting to grab Lady Eleen from their clutches, so we move fast to the trees then nice and quiet until we near the camp, then swords out and we rush in, do you all understand?" the troop responded "Yes Captain" with that they set off at a trot across the open field trampling the wheat as the sun slowly rose behind them.

Oswi and his small group stood ready also all sat astride their horses shields and swords at the ready Frik had a long knife strapped to his belt, he had strung his hunting bow, and had his arrows in hand he had explained to Oswi that if Lady Eleen was astride a horse with one of the men he would shoot the man and horse down so they could get to Lady Eleen easier. All was ready Bern would be moving in the time of action was close, and Oswi was sweating even though the morning had a chill to it. Ceoal was to his right and the remaining warriors strung out on either side all were excellent horsemen and skilled in battle. They all sat waiting patiently for Bern to start his noisy attack. Bern and the troop were now close to the camp of Lavos, they could see the cave through a break in the trees they could see people moving around. Bern looked at the troop spread out in a line across the wood, he smiled the time was now he gripped the reins of his horse and drew a breath "ATTACK" he shouted, and the troop jumped forward the men all shouting and screaming insults.

Lavos had been standing talking with Wigson when he heard the shout for the attack, "Quick get to your horses everyone, Wigson turned and grabbed Eleen who was sitting nearby roughly pulling her onto his horse and jumping up behind her, Lavos was astride his horse and the two set off to escape the rampaging troop of warriors. Beorn, Cernwulf, and Thornhed soon followed racing through the trees, the two recruits were not as quick and had not even got astride their horses before Bern and the others charged into the makeshift camp, both of them died with the swing of a sword as the troop charged through the camp following Lavos and the others.

Oswi and his section heard the shout of attack and gripped reins and swords ready they could hear the thunder of horses as Bern raced into the camp moments later they saw a group break cover of the trees Oswi saw Eleen astride a horse with Wigson and Lavos close by, Beorn, Cernwulf, Thornhed came as a second group all of them pushing their horses to escape. Oswi looked at his section "We go to Lady Eleen we must rescue her first" They all nodded Frik answered "I can take the horse down easily" Oswi looked at him "Are you sure ?" Frik did not answer he calmly drew the arrow and took aim he watched for mere moments before Oswi heard the whoosh of the arrow flying. Ceoal let out a whoop of joy as the arrow punched into the chest of the horse the blood sprayed up over Eleen the horse slowed, still running its heart gave out and collapsed to the ground. Oswi and the others raced forward Eleen had been thrown clear and Wigson was struggling to free himself from the horse, Lavos saw Eleen fall and slowed his horse to turn and grab her he saw Oswi and his men and faltered, snarling he whipped his horse and raced across the fields to escape.

. . .

CEOAL REACHED Eleen first he jumped from his horse to check her forgetting about Wigson who had managed to get free and was now striding towards them with seax in his hand., he only made four steps before Oswi thundered in on his horse and with swing of his sword chopped into Wigson's neck the warm sticky blood sprayed all over Oswi and his horse, Wigson was dead before his body hit the ground his life blood pumping from him turning the field red around him. Oswi jumped from his horse and walked towards Eleen, Ceoal had cut the bonds at her wrists, and she sat on the floor on seeing Oswi she jumped up and hugged him despite the blood over his face and mail "You came for me" she sobbed, and collapsed into Oswi's arms, he gently laid her down, looking at Ceoal "Bring some water she has fainted, it will be a delay to her been taken captive" Bern and the remainder of the troop arrived, Oswi stood and looked around "Any problems Bern?" Bern shook his head "Not one, just one injury some idiot forgot to duck under a branch, we killed the two recruits of friend Lavos, I see and Beorn, Cernwulf, and Thornhed escaped are we going after them?" Oswi looked down at Eleen, no they will be too close to Wrexham I dare not risk it we do not have enough men, no we must satisfy ourselves we rescued Eleen, it irks me that they are still free and alive, but I cannot risk the whole troop, no we make haste to get back to Holt and over the river to home" Bern nodded "We have the horses of the two dead men, Eleen can use one of those, what about him" enquired Bern as he kicked the body of Wigson. "Leave him for the crows and beasts, let us return home." Eleen was conscious again and Oswi helped her onto a horse and assigned Ceoal to ride next to her. "We need to make haste back to Farndon men; we do not wish to tarry long here in Powys" With that he turned his horse and set off.

. . .

THE RETURN TRIP luckily was uneventful, and the troop soon reached Holt and crossed the Old Roman bridge to safely return to Farndon. Oswi and the King's Troop received raucous cheers from Aruth and the warriors, Ethane came running fusing over Eleen. Oswi dismounted Vern was close to hand to take the horse from him. Aruth and Rolf appeared and spoke with Oswi and Bern to find out what had happened. Bern dismissed the troop and he returned to Crag Rock, Oswi went to his quarters to get cleaned up after all there was still work to do.

CHAPTER 17
THE TRAITOR LAVOS

Lavos was standing talking with Wigson about the route they would take to Wrexham when he heard the shout for the attack he turned looking through the trees he could see armed men on horseback approaching, he turned to his men "Quick get to your horses, everyone." Wigson turned and roughly grabbed Eleen who was sitting nearby quickly pulling her onto his horse and jumping up behind her. Lavos was soon astride his horse and they both kicked their horses to move so they could escape the rampaging troop of warriors. Beorn, Cernwulf, and Thornhed soon followed racing through the trees after Lavos and Wigson. Cernwulf glanced over his shoulder as his horse reached the tree line the two new men had been slow to react and were easily caught and killed, he kicked his horse to move faster. Beorn and Thornhed slowed and Cernwulf caught the two friends up "It is Bern and the King's troop, they caught the two new men and slaughtered them easily, we need to move" Beorn looked around "Lavos is there in front with Wigson" they set off to catch them up Thornhed quickly spoke "Look it is Oswi and some others in front" The three men watched as Oswi and his men raced towards Lavos and Wigson the old woodsman drew his bow and shot an arrow into the chest of Wigson's horse both he and Eleen tumbled from the horse the men watched as Lavos turned his horse abandoning both Wigson and Eleen.

WIGSON JUMPED to his feet after the horse was killed and drew his blade he could see the bastard Oswi thundering towards him, sword drawn and poised for an attack, Wigson was killed in an instant and fell dead to the floor. Oswi jumped clear of his horse and along with the others rushed to Lady Eleen. Bern and the King's Troop arrived, Bern watched as Lavos, and his remaining warriors spurred their horses across the fields towards a small wooden bridge over a stream. They covered the distance swiftly escape and safety was the only thing on their minds.

Lavos pulled his horse to a stop as it started to slow due to the frantic race away from the King's men and the bloody interfering Oswi. The others slowed behind him all now desperately wanted men. This had not gone as Lavos had planned. He looked at the men who had heads down looking sullen as they had no prospects. Cernwulf stopped at the far side of the bridge and shouted to the others "Slow down, they are not giving chase" Lavos stopped his horse and turned looking across the field he could see Oswi and his men in the distance all grouped together, he stood watching them for some time and then smiled as they turned as one to head back towards Holt then home.

ONCE THEY COULD SEE that Oswi and his men had gone from sight Lavos, and his small band crossed the bridge and slowly trudged back. They soon arrived at the body of Wigson, he had been left where he fell, and his horse a short distance away lay dead too.

Lavos looked at the body of his oldest friend Wigson, he had known him for many years and they had many adventures, Wigson had always stood by Lavos no matter what and helped keep the unit together he had a great mind and they had always been successful and had money due to the scheming of Wigson, that would be no more, Wigson had thrown his last dice and paid the ultimate price. Cernwulf jumped down from his own horse and stripped Wigson of his weapons deftly checking Wigson over and removing a bag of coins from within his mail. Beorn was knelt checking over the saddle and bags strapped to Wigson's horse, he removed a bag of food, and he found a further bag of coins.

THE SMALL BAND headed back to the camp from the previous night they needed to see if they could salvage any equipment and supplies as they would be needed.

Thornhed went first quietly and slowly into the camp to make sure that Oswi had not left men behind to capture them, all was still in the camp, and the bodies of their comrades both lay dead undisturbed from where they had fallen. Thornhed quickly signalled to his friends, and they all slowly ventured into the camp. They all dismounted and set to tasks, checking the dead, and collecting weapons and food all four of them were soon engrossed in their tasks, none heard the stealthy approach of a larger band of warriors that slunk in through the trees to surround the group.

UNKNOWN TO BOTH Oswi and Lavos the Powy's tribal leader in the area had been watching them all wondering what was happening. His scouts had advised him of two groups of Mercian warriors on his land, he had quickly assembled his warriors to head out and see for himself what the problem was. Now Chief Bledri and his second Rathan stood in the trees watching Lavos and his small band. Rathan stepped out from the shadows of the trees he stood in the open for all to see, Lavos and his band carried on sorting everything out unaware of the body of deadly men of Powy's all eagerly watching them. Bledri nodded at Rathan who both spoke English having lived so long on the border. "Who are you to enter the realm of Chief Bledri without invitation." Cernwulf turned with sword drawn to look into the trees, Lavos and Thornhed appeared in the mouth of the cave and Beorn stood up from the two dead comrades. It was Lavos who answered, " We are heading to Wrexham to seek employment as warriors" Lavos looked around the trees he needed to be careful he could see at least sixteen shadows in the trees, which meant there would be more men hidden deeper in the shadows.

"My name is Lavos, and these are my trusted warriors, who are you?"

Rathan stood boldly with his hands on his hips "I am Rathan champion of our Chief Bledri, who was the band of warriors that attacked you?"

Lavos needed to be careful now they had obviously been watched for some time, "They are warriors of the Thane of Farndon on the river Dee, we would not agree to be sworn to his service so when we left they chased us and killed two of our friends that lay here."

Rathan turned to Bledri and spoke in their singsong of Welsh; they both knew that Lavos was lying. Bledri had been informed that the raiders had taken over Wrexham and were going to war with the Mercians over the border. Bledri and Rathan spoke of this, they knew the Mercians were heading to Wrexham to join forces with the raiders it could be an opportunity for Bledri to join his forces with them and gain land and riches. Rathan agreed and turned to Lavos. "We will go with you to Wrexham, Chief Bledri asks that you introduce him to the raiders, if you do he will provide you food, weapons, and shelter and see you safely to the raiders." Lavos looked round at his small band they didn't really have much choice, "We agree." He said loudly

Rathan approached the camp with Bledri and soon all his warriors filtered down through the trees. Cernwulf did not feel comfortable with the current situation though he knew they did not have a choice. Cernwulf stood with Thornhed and Beorn and the three quickly counted up Chief Bledri had a warband of thirty warriors not including himself and his senior warrior Rathan, they all looked mean and nasty with an array of weapons and armour. Beorn spoke to his friends "We could do well here, with this group heading to Wrexham with us, maybe with Jarl Bjorn's men we could have enough warriors to attack Farndon and make it our own as we had originally planned." Thornhed usually quietly answered "We must stay alert though I trust not these men of Powys, keep your swords sharp and your mouths shut we cannot afford to anger them before we reach the safety of Wrexham.

The groups camped for the night in the trees and the cave. Bledri arranged for his men to assist with the burial of Wigson and the others. He also sent men back to his nearest village for ale and food for the whole group that evening. The men of Bledri and Mercia drank long into the night and arose late the next morning before breaking camp and heading out of the trees across the fields to the small wooden bridge. Once across the bridge, Bledri advised that they had crossed into a rival chief's land, and all needed to be cautious from here in until they reached Wrexham. Lavos was pleased with himself as now when he arrived at Wrexham he would have brought a warband with him, he may have lost his hostage, but he hoped Jarl Bjorn would be impressed with his new allies.

CHAPTER 18
THE TRAITOR SIGMUND

Sigmund had travelled home after the Lords Alestan and Ludeca had informed him the brat Oswi was the King's Commander in the King's Absence. Sigmund knew time was short he needed to get home and see which of his warriors would now stay loyal to him. Weeks passed and a summons arrived for him to attend the King at Farndon as a new Thane was to be appointed and the King requested his Lords to cast a vote. Sigmund was surprised that no mention of his failure to support the King was issued, so he decided to seek out the King. Sigmund anticipated that once the king was well enough to travel he would have visited Ealdorman Sigmund and denounce him as Ealdorman.

Sigmund arrived for the king's summons and was angered further when the King refused him an audience and then was asked to vote on promoting the young whelp Oswi to Thane. The King left the next morning heading north, leaving a message that Sigmund should return home and the King would call upon him soon. Sigmund left feeling despondent he did not the warriors to challenge the King directly on his own.

Sigmund needed allies, he was aware that Farndon's captain was causing dissent, was he in league with the Jarl Bjorn who almost had the King, hung, drawn, and quartered but for the timely arrival of the boy Oswi? He was a lucky warrior yes he was skilled, but his father Ealdorman Ludeca had managed to obtain him a position within the King's Guard and soon he had made himself invaluable to the King.

Sigmund summoned a trio of warriors all scum who he had often berated for being undisciplined but now these were the type of men he needed. He sent them to contact Jarl Bjorn to see if Ealdorman Sigmund would be welcome at his table and if would welcome him as an ally against King Offa. Sigmund needed to be sure he would be safe entering Bjorn's domain. Meanwhile, Sigmund arranged for his captain to seek out those who would remain loyal to him if the King came calling, Sigmund knew some men would falter and decide to step away from him if the King attacked. Sigmund had no family he had married years ago, and his wife had died during childbirth killing his son, he didn't care that she had died she had been useless and miserable, but it had rocked him to the core when his newborn baby son only lived mere moments.

Sigmund had vented his anger and frustration on the slaves and women who had been with his wife and son, one slave had died after he had stabbed her through the heart. He had become, sullen after the deaths, it was then he spent his time whoring, drinking, and fighting. He then had to spend time raiding over the border into Wessex and Powy's killing, and stealing, as he needed money he had spent so much money drinking. Sigmund had become excellent at raiding and soon attracted more men and took on larger raids. Soon he had boats and raided further afield striking at villagers along the coast round towards Northumberland and across to Ireland. He had become rich by buying more warriors all led by greed. The Kings before Offa knew of the raids and problems Sigmund caused but as he could field a large warband and the Kings always needed warriors they allowed him to continue with his raids.

THE BETRAYAL

. . .

KING OFFA HAD PROVED DIFFICULT, no matter what Sigmund offered in money or warriors the King wanted more, he discouraged the raids and informed Sigmund to treat with his neighbours and form trade agreements with them and allow merchants free trade and passage. Sigmund had ignored the King but then the summons to bring his warband to join the King's men as they needed to expel the raiders of Jarl Bjorn from Mercia. This was where the problem started as Sigmund had been allowing the Jarl access across his land to raid deep into Mercia and beyond. The agreement had been that Sigmund's land would be left untroubled and gold would be supplied to him to keep his warriors home and away from the Jarl's men. This had been going on for months and Sigmund was all the richer he had even allowed Jarl Bjorn to build a fortified settlement to enable him to attack deeper in the land. When Sigmund had joined with the King it was he that sent word to the Jarl, and he who did not bring his men to assist the King when the Jarl attacked.

SIGMUND PACED his hall he had arranged for some of his gold to be hidden and sent some men towards the border of Mercia and Powy's they had been told to find a suitable location and build a temporary fortified building. Sigmund had decided he would not wait for the King to come calling he intended to withdraw to a safe place somewhere he could retreat to a good secure stronghold. Sigmund had therefore sent men and weapons to the location. Sigmund was aware that the King was now recovered, and he knew it would not be long before he arrived. It was time to move he called his faithful hound of a Captain,

"You called for me my Lord," asked Mord as he entered the hall "Ah yes Mord it is time we left the hall, gather your loyal hounds, we know the King is fit and well I feel we have overstayed our time here in Mercia and need to seek adventure elsewhere" Mord smiled "Yes my Lord, do we head to out to the new fortification on the border" Sigmund turned walking to his private chamber "Yes Mord we do have my horse ready we leave today" Mord turned and headed out of the hall to assemble the men, Mord had plans of his own for Sigmund he smiled as he went to prepare. Sigmund watched his hound leave the hall, he hoped he had gambled right.

SIGMUND WAS WALKING across the courtyard to collect his horse which stood ready next to Mord, who had assembled thirty stern, grim-faced warriors. Sigmund was pleased as twenty other warriors were already at the new fortification at the border with Powys. Mord passed the reins of his own and Sigmund's horse to a man standing nearby, he stepped out boldly towards Sigmund and drew his sword from his hip and his axe from his back. Sigmund stopped and looked hard at the scowling Mord "What are you doing man" Sigmund enquired. Mord looked around at his hounds who sat impassively waiting for the outcome grinning he replied "Change of management" Sigmund instantly realised Mord meant to kill him and take his gold and warriors; he deftly drew his own sword and seax from his belt and stood poised ready for battle. Sigmund was skilled but deep down he knew Mord was stronger faster and deadly in a fight. A few warriors stood on duty made to assist Sigmund, but he waved them back they would die needlessly as Mord had the advantage of numbers.

MORD DID NOT SPEAK as he strode out to meet Sigmund hefting his sword and axe he jumped forward swinging the axe towards Sigmund's head and the sword swung towards his stomach, Sigmund twisted and ducked then stabbed out with his sword in response. Both men circled each other each attacking then defending neither scoring a hit against the other sword clanged on the sword seax deflected the axe. Mord's strength in his attacks was felt hard by

Sigmund it vibrated through his body, he knew he could not keep up fighting Mord for much longer as his attacks grew weaker as his hands and arms were now numb from the impacts of the blade on blade, where Mord's attacks had not faltered. Everyone was engrossed in the sword fight in the yard and nobody apart from the gate sentries was aware that the King had arrived with a large group of his warriors. The gate sentries quickly opened the gate and sullenly advised the King that their Captain and some of the troops were rebelling against Ealdorman Sigmund. King Offa slowly walked his horse through the gate and watched as Sigmund fell to his knees once more as the huge captain slammed his sword down with tremendous force with an overhead swing.

King Offa spoke with his troops who moved their horses around behind the watching warriors then with Ealdorman Ludeca and Alestan he moved forward he spoke with Alestan who smiled drawing a throwing spear from his saddle he took aim. The spear shot from his meaty grip and flew straight and true slamming into the back of Mord between his shoulders the force was such that the point exploded out of his chest splattering blood and gore over the kneeling form of Sigmund. Mord looked at the bloody spear point in his chest his arms went limp weapons thudding to the packed earth of the courtyard. Mord stood swaying coughing blood up he staggered and fell to the floor. Sigmund stayed knelt down and dropped his weapons from aching arms it was then he noticed the King and hated him with every inch of his body, the King had saved him which hurt more than losing to Mord. Mord's chosen warriors stepped horses forward some drawing blades, none had noticed the King's troops behind them. Ealdorman Ludeca had been stationed to watch the group of warriors on seeing the open threat to the King by drawing swords he waved his arm and the King's troop attacked.

. . .

LAUNCHING their horses forward they ran spears through the closest of the treacherous warriors dispatching half their number as easily as drawing breath. The remaining warriors turned to fight the King's troops but were outnumbered three to one. The battle was over as quickly as it had started and none of Mord's men were left alive, bodies lay slumped over horses or had dropped to the courtyard. The King's troops had not even broken a sweat, and none had been injured. They soon bent to the tasks of disposing of the bodies. The King and his Lords now stood in front of the still kneeling Sigmund his chest still heaved from the onslaught he had faced from the dead Mord. King Offa strode off towards Sigmund's hall with Ludeca and Alestan to nobody in particular he shouted, "Bring this idiot to the hall, we will speak with him" Alestan motioned to a group of troops who jumped to the task of escorting Sigmund rather than heave dead bodies around. The King sat in Ealdorman Sigmund's chair within his hall Ealdorman Ludeca and Alestan stood either side of him as the troops half carried half dragged Ealdorman Sigmund across the hall dropping him a short distance from the feet of the King.

"Stand up man" shouted King Offa, grimacing Sigmund slowly stood, he was sheened in sweat from his battle with Mord his chest still heaved from the exertions, he did not look at the King, he dared not as the murder was in his mind and he knew the King would kill him in a heartbeat if he looked, did or said anything untoward at this time. Sigmund slowed his breathing down to calm himself he forced himself to stand straight and tall then raised his head to acknowledge the King. King Offa looked at the man in front of him, he knew he had schemed and allowed the raiders to cross his land. How deep his disloyalty went he did not know but the King trusted him not and now was the time to sort this scum of a Lord out once and for all.

" EALDORMAN SIGMUND," Offa said formally, "You stand here accused of cowardice and not aiding your Lord and King in battle, you have spent years raiding across our borders causing problems with our neighboring kingdoms and profiting from their misfortune, we arrive today to find you have also lost control of your troops and find you in what looked like a fight to the death, what have you to say?"

Sigmund looked at the King and the two Lords, he was unsure what to say though knew he must answer the King. "My Lord King, I must thank you for your timely arrival, I had been informed you were close by and had my men ready as we planned to ride and meet you enroute" a total fabrication but Sigmund hoped it sounded good he continued "My captain as you saw had my men under his control and sought to kill me and usurp the lands I own by your leave." Sigmund continued "They had previously disobeyed me," "ENOUGH of your lies" shouted the King, "Sigmund we know you allowed Jarl Bjorn to raid across the lands of Mercia and did nothing to stop him other lesser Lords tried and did not have the troops and failed which is why I was forced to act I took you with me in the hope you would show some back bone and loyalty to me and Mercia, but you failed, you also failed in controlling your own household troops and managing your estates. THEREFORE, I have spoken with the other leading Lords, and we are all in agreement." The King stopped and looked at Ealdorman Alestan to continue the King was red faced and furious. Sigmund stood still and unmoving. Ealdorman Alestan now spoke on behalf of King Offa "Lord Sigmund, you stand before your King and peers, accused of cowardice and disloyalty to your King and the realm of Mercia, hence forth you will be Lord no longer within the Kingdom of Mercia, you will forfeit your hall and estates, your men will be yours no more, you have ten days to leave the realm of Mercia, the King has deemed you to be unfit to stay, you may take your horse, armour and weapons only and never return, if you do you will be hung as a common criminal. Do you understand this Sigmund?"

Sigmund's head dropped it was over he smiled inside or so the King thought the idiot did not know he had a troop of loyal warriors and gold he would go seek out Jarl Bjorn and form an alliance.

Ealdorman Alestan spoke the Kings troops "Take him from here get him on his horse and out the gate away from your King." The men grabbed Sigmund hauling him out the hall and threw him across his horse kicking it and laughing as it bolted out of the gate and down the road, hopefully never to be seen again in Mercia.

King Offa looked at Alestan and Ludeca "It is done, Alestan send word to your eldest ask him to come here and take temporary control of Sigmund's former hall and estates. We will decide at a meeting with the other Lord's as who we will give the lands to, but for now he can act in my stead here, it will help him when he finally gets to take on your mantel." Alestan laughed "I hope you do not think I am leaving you anytime soon Sire? Still life in this old dog yet and I can still swing a sword" The King smiled and replied "Aye, do not worry, I still have need of your services my friend, you and Ludeca can stay with me a while longer, Let us have an ale we deserve it, thirsty work evicting scum" The three old friends laughed with each other.

CHAPTER 19
THE ENEMY

Life went on as normal around Farndon and Crag Rock. Crag Rock was rebuilt with a small fence around the compound of buildings making it more secure. Farndon's gates were completed they were now taller and stronger and had a strong fighting platform around them. Bern along with Ceoal supervised the improvements of the wall surrounding Farndon which was nearly finished and stood half the height again with a sturdy walkway and platform its full length. In addition, large, pointed stakes had been placed where the ground to the wall was a gentle slope to discourage any attack from there. Oswi had also instructed that the track to the gate and the area in front be larger and wider and clear of trees and shrubs that may cover any attacking force.

THE TRACK that led down to the river was also widened and cleared the small jetty and moorings had all been moved so any boats could anchor closer to the Old Roman bridge where sentries now stood guard day and night. Bern along with Brak the Smith had spent time at the old watchtower at the far end of the bridge, they had managed to rebuild some of the stone of the tower and added a wooden lookout post on top to guard the bridge and river. The watchtower would be hard to attack as stakes had been placed all around its base and you could only reach the lookout post if a rope was thrown down to climb up. Oswi had also arranged for a stockpile of lightweight throwing spears, hunting bows and arrows, and piles of rocks along with brands soaked in tar to light up if any attack came from Powys. Oswi's only problem had been guards and warriors. Lan had recovered to take over from Wulfure and had proven very capable and experienced the section he led was proud to have him he wore a purple braid in his long hair a personal gift from Eleen on her return. Aruth had ventured out twice during the previous weeks to recruit more men, Lan, Wareson, Drom and Alfe all now commanded nine men each and Aruth had a group of eight young men who ran errands and helped cook and look after the horses these men were also training in weapons as replacements should they be required. Oswi now commanded over forty warriors at Farndon and a further twenty of the King's troop based at Crag Rock, he also had other men in the village and surrounding small holdings he could call on if required, and he could field a warband of around seventy-five experienced warriors. Rolf had provided a recent update and trade was flowing well through Farndon and beyond, boats paid fees to land at Farndon, and fees to load and unload goods Farndon's chest had never been so full. Oswi was pleased with how everything had progressed, Farndon was a happy thriving place, and Crag Rock was producing excellent crops and had laughter once more from the families. The men were all trained, Brak had done an excellent job with the new smiths, and weapons were made and stored for the King.

THE NEW BAKER was very popular in the village, and most of all Oswi was spending time with Eleen. They talked some evenings until late discussing how life for the villagers could be further improved, Oswi found it easy to talk with Eleen his feelings for her had grown since the rescue, Oswi was going to speak with the King when next they met about Eleen. He desired her hand in marriage but as she was a ward of the King it was to him he must obtain approval.

The next morning when Oswi met as usual with Bern, Ceoal, Rolf, and Aruth, to hear the reports. Aruth advised that the watchtower had seen riders during the night, they had not approached the tower, the men on duty had counted at least twelve on horseback and were sure that more men were on foot. Oswi listened to the report and looked at Bern "Assemble the King's troop for me, armour, shields, weapons, and spears, we will go out past Holt to look for signs, ask Frik if he will join us, Ceoal you too, Aruth & Rolf can watch Farndon while we are out checking the area." Bern responded, "You suspect an attack?" Oswi's face was calm, "I am not sure it could be just some Welshmen looking to cross into Mercia to cause mayhem, but we need to check out the size of the party, we cannot risk a fight out in the open with a larger force" "I agree" answered Bern "Why do we not look to build a barricade across the road next to the watchtower, that way it could hamper anyone coming towards the bridge from Holt but leave the bridge open for us to support the watchtower if anything happens" "Yes, good idea, Aruth can you set men to undertake the task, a few good sized stones pulled up from the side of the river with branches and sharpened stakes should deter them, also we need a signal fire across there and extra firebrands" replied Oswi "I will see to that we will leave a rock to one side so you can pass back through easily later today" suggested Aruth. "Good idea, let us eat and be about our tasks men, another busy day ahead for us" laughed Oswi.

Later that morning Oswi, along with Bern rode out with the King's troop, Ceoal had left earlier with Frik and one trooper to allow Frik to check the tracks over and try to make sense of them. They headed over the bridge Oswi noticed men already pulling large rocks up the river bank to block the road others, followed across the bridge with stockpiles of weapons for the watchtower. Oswi turned in his saddle and looked across at the small wood beyond Farndon he could see men chopping down trees presumably for the barricade and to make more wooden spikes. The men on duty in the watchtower waved as they rode past. Frik had gone past Holt and followed a similar path they had taken when searching for Lady Eleen. Frik did not like this it did not feel right something was wrong. He stopped and looked at the tracks they crisscrossed backward and forwards over the fields to and from Holt, Frik held his hand up and looked around a tall, lonely tree stood off to his right he climbed down from his pony and quickly ran over to the tree nimbly climbing it as high as he could, he looked around towards the hills and trees they had waited at before and back to the river twisting away from Holt further inland behind them. Frik was back at his pony in a flash and spoke to Ceoal "If we go further we will be trapped, there are men at the hill across the field they are hidden in the boulders I saw a glint of the sun coming off weapons or armour, and others hide in the river bed behind us, we must go back"

The three men rode off meeting Oswi and the troop as they cleared the village of Holt, Oswi halted the troop seeing Frik and the others return, he was instantly concerned as they approached fast. Frik quickly apprised Oswi of the trap and where the warriors hid. Oswi could not be sure how many men would be there, so he withdrew back to the watchtower, warning the men on duty to stay alert.

HE SENT the troops back to gather more weapons and saw that Crag Rock was abandoned and everyone went to Farndon. The barricade was nearly completed. Oswi spoke with Bern and Ceoal "I want Alfe and his full section here on duty tonight, Alfe in the tower with three men and the others here at the barricade with lit torches, and some shrubs that will burn. If an attack comes I want the shrubs lit and then the men can join Alfe in the watchtower, it will be rather tight up there, but they should be safe and be able to throw spears, and arrows at any force crossing the bridge." Bern looked at the watchtower "Maybe we should have made it bigger" Oswi smiled "Too late now, I want the Kings troop split into two sections Bern you will command one and rest this night, Ceoal will command the other and take the night watch with Lan's section, that will leave Drom's and Wareson's section to rest as well, if possible Wareson will go out in the morning to relieve Alfe's section" Ceoal spoke we could arm the villagers as many of them are capable" Oswi nodded yes we can Aruth can command them they can be used if an attack comes until then it will be trained men only who stand watch" Bern and Ceoal nodded their understanding they could not risk any untrained man getting caught out and no alarm raised. Oswi looked around "Back to Farndon, we need to get organised."

THE ATTACK CAME in the dead of night, it started at the watchtower. Alfe heard rather than saw the attackers, the creak of leather the jingle of weapons, and the smell of sweat assailed his sensors, he climbed down to warn the men at the barricade to listen out, Frik had advised them to throw small dry twigs and leaves across the road a short distance in front of the barricade he explained to Alfe if he listened he would hear the attackers step on the twigs making them snap and the leaves would rustle. This was now what the men at the barricade listened for once they heard it they would light the shrubs and retreat up the watchtower using the ropes slung down ready for them.

ONE OF THE section heard the first snap of a twig he turned and nodded to the others who quickly lit the shrubs, the men quickly ran the half dozen steps to climb the ropes up the watchtower the last man stood at the bottom when the first attacker came running from the darkness swords rang as they clashed a second and third attacker arrived and the guard was soon hard pressed Alfe watched as he took a wound to his shoulder, he looked at the rest of his section "pull the ropes up we cannot help him now" Alfe continued to watch as the guard attacked again, he sliced the neck of one attacker before a sword took him from behind. Alfe ordered the men to throw spears at the attackers as they climbed over and around the barricade they looked to be around forty attackers surging around the watchtower this was looking ugly. Alfe's section rained the light throwing spears down on the attacking warriors at the base of the watchtower. The attackers were not expecting the barrage of missiles from above.

ALFE WATCHED as his section threw a second time roughly a dozen attackers were down not all were killed some struggled to pull spears free or drag themselves away bleeding as they did. Trik a recruit to Alfe's section stood grabbed a third spear and hefted it into the attackers, he threw hastily completely missing his target, The lean warrior he aimed at swiftly collected the spear from the ground by his feet poised himself and drew back his arm the spear shot out at speed catching Trik full in the chest. Blood sprayed over his fellow guards the force of the throw had sent the spear through his body and the head was clearly showing out of his back. Trik let out a soft groan and tumbled from the watchtower to land in a bloody heap at the base alongside the attacking dead and wounded. Alfe groaned a young life snatched away he turned to his remaining men "Take care, be sure of your target we cannot afford for them to use our weapons against us men, he turned to the four closest to him you four grab your bows, fire at any who try to head to the bridge" the men quickly acted on the Alfe's orders and stood at the corner nearest the bridge. It was then that one of the men shouted Alfe "Alfe, look they have boats they are crossing the river" Alfe quickly stood and looked where the man pointed around six small boats and rafts were crossing just up river from them they must have stolen the craft from Holt and now used them to get more men across the river to attack Farndon. Alfe looked at the men "Do you think you could hit any of them?" two men leaned over the edge of the watchtower one spoke after looking at his companion "If we are quick, we may catch a few on the last boat, but these bows are not big enough for a long distance" Alfe held up his hand "No do not try then, concentrate on those we can easily kill here and trying to cross the bridge"

ALFE TURNED AWAY and looked around the road and bridge area the attackers were currently concentrated around the broken-down barrier and the watchtower some hurling broken pieces of wood, stone, and the odd bent spear up at them so far no other defender had been injured or killed. Alfe saw a few attackers sprint for the bridge none made it, all ended up peppered with arrows and fell dead. Alfe looked across the river to Farndon he could see the glow of torches on the wall and the small silhouettes of the man on duty, he looked across once more as he saw a light appear, what was it? He looked hard staring out across the dark expanse, he stood shocked when he suddenly realized what it was, someone had opened the small southern gate in the wall that led down a small hidden path through the rocks down towards the river. Alfe stood shocked someone inside Farndon had betrayed them. Who and why, Alfe stood his heart racing what could he do to warn Oswi and the others at Farndon, he gripped the wooden rail hard as he stood watching, sweat poured from him he turned to one of the archers, "Grab some arrows and light them fire them as high up as you can into the air three as quick as you can, we need to warn Farndon someone has opened the southern gate" the man looked momentarily surprised then jumped into action.

. . .

Alfe turned to the rest of the men "Keep at it men get some more rocks and spears thrown at them, pick your targets" As the archer quickly organised himself Alfe looked around the watchtower once more, he did a quick count of the bodies eighteen by his calculation for two of his own men, they had done well so far.

CHAPTER 20
THE BETRAYAL

Ceoal was walking the perimeter of the wall with Lan as they checked the troops and guards on duty were all awake and alert, Bern had instructed them to be attentive as he felt sure any attack if it should come would be at night to try and surprise the defenders of the watchtower and Farndon. The other troops and guards were all resting but all had been given the message to stay dressed and have arms nearby. Ceoal and Lan had just completed the circuit and stood on the gateway looking out towards Crag Rock, still in deep conversation when Lan stopped and turned looking across Farndon towards the river, he held his hand up for Ceoal to remain quiet "Hush Ceoal, I am sure I heard something" he kept looking towards the river "Come Ceoal lets move around the wall I am unable to see the watchtower from here but I am sure I heard something" The two men set off walking towards the southern wall, Ceoal suddenly noticed the guard stationed at the corner of the east and southern wall was waving his hands "Lan quick, there is something happening" the two ran down the wall to the guard who spoke quickly "Look the watchtower there are men attacking the barricade and the tower" Ceoal and Lan looked on the men on duty had set the bushes alight and all it seemed had retreated to the tower it was too far away to be sure.

THEY COULD SEE shapes pulling the barricade apart to allow more attacking warriors through to the watchtower and bridge. Ceoal looked to the guard "Go and rouse Aruth, ask him to request he Bern and Thane Oswi attend us here at your post." The guard ran the wall to the nearest ladder and quickly descended running across the village to Aruth's hut. Ceoal and Lan continued to look out across to the watchtower, Ceoal spoke "Lan I will leave you here to keep watch and await the others I will quickly go to each guard and check and advise them to be very alert and call out if they see anything this could be a diversion" Lan replied, "Yes good idea Ceoal, you are right, we need to check the whole perimeter, I will advise Lord Oswi if you have not returned." Ceoal set off leaving Lan watching looking out he hoped Alfe and his section were all safe.

Ceoal returned to the wall after checking with the other guards to find Lord Oswi already there, he was looking out towards the watchtower with Lan and Bern when he turned hearing Ceoal's footsteps "Ah Ceoal is everything all right around the rest of the wall" "Yes Oswi, no problems" replied Ceoal.

Oswi turned back to look across the river, "It looks like Alfe, and his men are in the watchtower the warriors are breaking the barrier apart and it looks like they have attacked the watchtower, and a few tried to run for the bridge recently but did not make it" Aruth arrived on the wall "The men are getting ready Oswi, I have instructed them to assemble in the courtyard as you suggested" "Thank you Aruth, I think we just need to be alert and see what happens now"

Lan was standing leaning over the top of the wall, "I think we have a problem" Oswi stood next to him and peered over the wall to where Lan was pointing, Oswi turned to the others "The southern gate is open"

. . .

THE BETRAYAL

THEY ALL STOOD LOOKING at each other, Ceoal moved first running to the nearest ladder Aruth close behind him, Oswi, and Bern followed with Lan at the rear. Ceoal jumped off the ladder and quickly ran around the buildings towards the southern gate, Aruth launched himself into the air to jump to the ground and race after Ceoal. The others were still on top of the walkway. Ceoal raced towards the gate he could see it wide open, the torches from inside Farndon shone brightly like a star it would be making it very obvious to the attackers that a gate was open.

ARUTH SOON CAUGHT up with Ceoal and the pair were soon close to the gate a huge dark shadow stepped from outside the wall to block the gate, Ceoal and Aruth slowed to a walk when they saw who was standing there. "Drom, you're here, who opened the gate do you know" asked Aruth. Drom stood feet apart in the gateway and slowly drew a huge axe from a strap across his back from his waist he drew his sword both glinting with the flames of the torch-lit area.

Aruth stopped "Drom?" Drom stepped back inside the wall standing firmly to block the access "My friends, I am sorry you are the ones to come to the gate" Aruth looked to Ceoal with a puzzled expression, Ceoal frowned and shrugged his shoulders he too not understanding. Drom let out a deep sigh and took up a defensive warrior posture with his weapons held towards them. Drom momentarily dropped his head and then looked deep firstly into Aruth's eyes then Ceoal's meanwhile Oswi, Bern, and Lan were still running through the village towards the gate. Drom turned and looked down the narrow hidden pathway leading up from the river he could see Lavos with a torch leading the way he needed to hold the gate until they arrived, he set a grim-looking figure armed stood in the gate "The gate stays open" was all he said Ceoal looked to Aruth "Drom, oh no please no" Aruth did not understand what was happening and stepped forward Ceoal reached out and pulled him back as Drom swiftly swung the sharp axe at him, Aruth felt the axe swing by his face and quickly pulled his own sword out "DROM," he shouted "What is wrong." It was Ceoal who answered, "We are betrayed, Drom is here as he has opened the gate for the scum attacking us, the watchtower is a diversion to allow him the opportunity, I am right, Drom am I not?" Drom grinned "Well done young Ceoal quick as ever yes, I opened the gate, yes the men are coming here to the gate up the path, yes the watchtower was to give me time, though I did hope you would not see the open gate and come to look"

Ceoal drew his sword and his seax, Aruth had already drawn his sword, though he also drew his long hunting knife as the realization hit him they must kill Drom to shut the gate or die trying. Ceoal and Aruth stepped quickly to the attack Aruth from Drom's left with a high swing of his sword and a low strike with his knife, Ceoal attacked from the right he held his sword high as a defence and aimed to strike his seax into the forearm of Drom. They both failed Drom was very agile for a big man he swung his sword round fast and sure, clipping both Aruth's knife and sword and then lunging forward with his own attack causing Aruth to jump backwards, Ceoal's attack fared no better as the axe swung causing Ceoal to dip his head meaning his seax was nowhere near his intended target.

This was the site that greeted Oswi, Bern, and Lan as they ran the last stretch to the gate. Oswi shouted out annoyed "What is going on" Drom just grinned and swung the axe once more narrowly missing Ceoal's face and Aruth's chest. Oswi looked at Ceoal questionably Ceoal shrugged "Drom opened the gate, sir, the attackers are on the rock path" Lan reacted first drawing his knives from his belt he swiftly launched three in quick succession at Drom. Drom spun the first sliced his left ear the second he deflected with his axe but the third hit home in his shoulder. Aruth jumped forward stabbing out with his long hunting knife to strike Drom's leg as Ceoal struck out at his side once more. Aruth struck home but felt Drom's sword slice open his chainmail and back with his sword, Aruth dropped to the floor screaming in pain, Oswi stepped forward, but Lan and Bern dragged him back, it was Bern who shouted in Oswi's face "NO Oswi leave Drom we will assist, you must rally the men, all of them and form a defensive line here as if we fail to kill Drom and shut the gate then hell will arrive here very soon." Oswi looked at Bern he was annoyed that Drom had betrayed them, but knew Bern was right, he snarled a response "KILL HIM" and turned shouting for the troops and guards.

BERN TURNED to Lan both drawing weapons and stepping forward Ceoal was fighting for his life against the Drom the axe and sword reaching, searching, and stabbing out at him Ceoal was defending himself but stepping back each time he had lost his seax and now only had his sword. Aruth's back was sliced open from his right shoulder down across his back to his left hip, he had slowly crawled away but now lay not moving in the hard-packed dirt. Drom had two wounds, his shoulder and leg though neither was slowing down his strong attack against Ceoal. Lan slid in next to Ceoal deflecting the axe and stabbing a small throwing knife he had into the wrist of Drom, who let out a blood-curdling scream when it smashed into his wrist. Drom snatched his arm back wrenching the blade out of his wrist with his teeth, Bern attacked at this point sword and seax swinging fast and sure at Drom who took a pace back two red lines appeared through Drom's tunic as Bern sliced his blades over his chest. Drom spun reaching with his sword to hinder Bern he tried to swing his axe to meet the double attack from Lan and Ceoal but his wrist pumping out blood could no longer take the axe's weight and it tumbled from his numb fingers to the floor. Lan hit first a blade rammed into Drom's ribs, and Ceoal struck next slicing deep into Drom's already injured leg and causing him to fall to one knee. Drom swung his sword still fighting back causing Lan to jump back and Ceoal to roll away. Drom laughed a deep loud booming laugh that seemed to shake the walls he knew he was beaten but could still attack and maim people, he had just started a swing back towards Bern who was reaching once more for him, when he felt an immense pain sear through his chest he dipped his head and looked down as he saw the point of a blade punch out through his chest its point bright red sprayed the ground in front of him with more blood. He coughed and blood filled his mouth, groaning he dropped to his other knee, the blade was slowly pulled from his chest making a grotesque wet slurping sound as it was withdrawn. Drom looked up coughing again blood splattering his chest and the ground each time Lan, Ceoal, and Bern all stood in front of him weapons held poised ready to continue the fight.

DROM WAS FINISHED he could hear the approach of the attacking warriors as they scrambled up the wet slippery, rocky path, had he held the gate long enough? It didn't matter really now as he was dying, and he would not be rewarded with the promised gold. He looked up once more and could see Thane Oswi approaching with the men and armed villagers, Drom thought to himself picked the wrong side as Aruth appeared directly behind him blood running down his injured back, his hunting knife sheened with Drom's blood. Aruth's face was set with determination as he gripped the hair of Drom pulling his head back and slicing the hunting knife across Drom's throat. Drom gurgled and spluttered falling dead to the floor. Aruth steeped around him walking towards the others each step jarred his back and sent pain shooting through his body.

BERN LOOKED over his shoulder to see Oswi and the men mere steps away. And turned back to the others "Quick the gate" it was too late.
    Bern, Ceoal, Lan, and the wounded Aruth felt they had failed as the area around the gateway slowly filled with men at the front of

the group stood Lavos, smiling cruelly. Lavos kicked the body of Drom over taking a step closer to the men of Farndon.

"Not quick enough, friend Aruth, though I must thank you for killing the big idiot we will not have to pay him now, will we have more for us."

Oswi pushed through his loyal friends and Captains he saw Lavos, armed and ready to fight, tonight would be a brutal, bloody night, with no quarter given. They must fight for the very survival of Farndon.

CHAPTER 21
THE FIGHT FOR FARNDON

The attackers continued to spill into the inner confines of Farndon through the gate opened by the warrior Drom who had betrayed his Thane, his friends, and the people of Farndon.

Lavos stood at the front of the attacking warriors who seemed to be a mix of Raiders, Welsh, and Mercian warriors. Oswi was puzzled as to why such a mix of warriors, he had presumed that Lavos had been in league with the raiders but could not understand why he could see so many Mercian warriors.

IT WAS THEN he heard a voice, a voice he knew. "Move, out of my way, why are we not moving? this place should be full of screaming and wailing by now, move you lazy bastards, move" A tall slim, long in the face with long dark hair pushed through the warriors he was clad in black armour and held a black shield. He stood next to Lavos, he gave a sneer of a smile "Oh the boy leader, is here, good, good" Oswi nodded his head smiling at the recently exiled Sigmund, "Sigmund the Snake, I see you are in good company, well we know who has been behind it all now!"

Sigmund sneered at Oswi, "Well you may know but the knowledge will die with you and all here in Farndon, we have plenty of friends here to help us."

THE TWO GROUPS of warriors stood facing each other with swords, shields, axes and spears all ready, nobody moved, Lavos and Sigmund had both stepped back behind their warriors. Oswi stood with Bern on his left, Lan to his right Aruth stood behind him and the Guards of Farndon had fanned out left and right to make the first line of the shield wall. The king's troop stood behind and made the second line, Ceoal had moved to stand with these men to hold them and use them to fill the gaps that would soon appear in the front line.

BRAK THE SMITH had rallied the abled-bodied men of Farndon and had these stood ready to assist. Ceoal had sent the youths who assisted Aruth up to the wall and told them to drop firebrands, rocks, and anything they could find down onto the attackers stood in the gateway. The attackers started banging swords and axes on shields lots of warriors did this to stir themselves into battle some drank to gain bravery. It was no mean thing to charge a shield wall bristling with weapons. Oswi instructed his men to stay quiet he hoped that if his men stood calm and still it would unnerve the attacking warriors.

Oswi stood shield in front and sword in hand. He could still hear shouts and cries of pain carry over the river, he smiled Alfe was still causing problems for anyone trying to cross the bridge and at least he knew some of the men of Farndon were still alive at the watchtower.

Oswi was jabbed in the ribs by Bern, "They will be on us soon, stand ready we lead the men today."

· · ·

Sigmund and Lavos were both growing impatient shouting shoving and pushing the warriors to attack a few stepped forward and shouted at their comrades to come with them. Slowly they stepped forward to form a line once more. Then a step at a time they moved forward as one. Bern looked around at the men and shouted, "First line lock shields"

The wooden shields clashed together swords rasped from sheaths, and men firmly planted their feet to await the crash of the two walls then the pushing slashing, and stabbing would begin.

The attackers stepped on, then straightened their line and crashed into the first line of Oswi's defence the shields creaked the men groaned as the attackers pushed and pushed against them. "Hold" shouted Bern, "Hold them men."

Above on the wall, the youths rained lit firebrand stones and lumps of timber down onto attacking warriors near the gate. Lady Eleen and some other older men joined them they threw spears and shot arrows at the attackers killing some and wounding others who fell from the rear lines of the attackers. Ceoal had been busy organising the King's troop he had sent Brak and the other smiths into the stables where some of the new heavy spears had been stored ready to be transported down to Crag Rock. Ceoal had passed the spears out amongst the King's troop with instructions that he would shout when the time was right to use the spears.

Ceoal stood watching as the two lines slammed together the noise echoed around the buildings, drumming in his ears. The attackers threw themselves at the wall punching shields forward to try and slam the men of Farndon back, swords, and axes rained down on helms and shoulders on each line causing men to fall or step back from the line. The floor would soon become wet and slippery with the blood and excrement of the men fighting. Ceoal heard Lavos and

Sigmund shouting at the men and pushing them on. Ceoal waited he wanted them to commit more men to the front of the shield wall, the idea he had would have a bigger impact with a larger body of men opposing them.

THE ATTACKERS PUSHED, smashed shields into shields, and pushed again. The men of Farndon were holding a few men who had fallen to the rear with wounds. Oswi was the focus of a few attacks, he had fended these off striking the first man through his mouth as he screamed at him blood showering the other attackers. The second had smashed an axe into Oswi's shield trying to wrench it from his grasp as a third reached out with his sword Bern and Lan soon dispatched them both. They made a small barrier of bodies on the floor though these were soon stamped on again and again as the men pushed in the shield wall. Sigmund pushed more men into the wall shouting for them to push, the attackers had nearly double the amount of men in the front line of the wall than the defenders of Farndon. Swords and axes reached out trying to snatch the lives of the defenders. They held the line but were finding it more and more difficult to hold back the tide of attackers.

OSWI AND BERN shouted encouragement to the men. The youths and old men still rained spears and arrows down onto the men at the rear of the attacking force. Ceoal strained to look over the heads of the men of Farndon, he could see them sweating and pushing to hold the line firm, he could see that at least two-thirds of the attacking force was now committed to the shield wall, now was the time for his plan to come into action. Ceoal joined the men of the King's troop picking up his own large-headed spear newly made, sharpened, and glinting from the flaming torches around the walls. These killing weapons had yet to be blooded, but here, now, on this dark night, the spears would kill and maim the attackers the blades would soon be awash with blood, spilling it like a flood onto the dry ground.

CEOAL LEANED FORWARD and spoke to Oswi "Get ready" Oswi quickly turned looked at Ceoal and knocked the arm of both Bern and Lan, so they too were now aware, and the message passed down the line of defenders in the front of the shield wall who were now close to breaking such was the pressure of the large group of attacking warriors.

CEOAL LOOKED down the line of King's troop and nodded "LIFT" he shouted and as one of the men hefted the heavy spears. "HOLD" was the next instruction, and the men took a step forward to balance the spears on the shoulders of the men in the first line. All was ready the attackers thrust forward again trying to push the defenders over such was the force of the attack a lot of them overstretched and were off balance. Both Oswi and Ceoal saw the opportunity and shouted "THRUST" Twelve heavy spears of death all virgins to the blood of enemies thrust forward, the blades were keen and sharp the attacker in front of Bern had no time to move or scream as the blade hit home in the middle of his face exploding his head like a soft melon blood, bone, and brain matter showered the men behind him as he dropped dead instantly to the floor. The man directly in front of Oswi was tall and covered in chain mail even that did not keep him safe, Oswi watched almost in slow motion as the spear thrust across his right shoulder the sharp point punching into the mail and the links splitting asunder as the head drove deeper and deeper into the warrior's chest right into his heart the man screamed momentarily but as the blade hit his heart smashing it easier than the links of chainmail the scream stopped as blood pumped out of the now gaping cavity of his chest. Elsewhere up and down the line the twelve heavy spears snatched a life from the attackers. One attacker who had slipped as he lunged forward had his life snatched the spear going through his groin the high-pitched wail he made was like a banshee screaming in the wind. Others had the blades smash through open mouths and into the soft tissue of an eye socket and sprayed blood and body parts over the defenders and the other attackers. The blades had tasted blood and needed more.

CEOAL SHOUTED AGAIN "HOLD" and the blades all swiftly withdrew from the bodies which fell and flopped to the floor making a barrier of death. The king's troop once more balanced the blades as the attackers screamed and shouted their frustrations at the defenders Lavos had seen from his position to the left of the line the deadly precision the king's troop had used the spears in. Lavos heard Sigmund shout at the men to move forward fresh men led by Jarl Bjorn pushed through having arrived late.

THEY WERE fresh and wanted blood they knocked the other attackers away to replace the front line they pushed hard against Oswi and his men. Ceoal knew he must use the spears once more or they could still lose the fight for Farndon. He looked at the King's troop who nodded they had all realised it too. Ceoal noticed the Jarl bashing two axes' into Oswi's shield and warriors on either side seeking to stab a blade into him. Ceoal drew breath "THRUST" he shouted and once more twelve spears shot forward to create more carnage. The raiders under Jarl Bjorn were more experienced and quicker a couple managed to duck behind raised shields these were smashed to pieces by the heavy spear blade.

ONE DUCKED to have the blade miss him completely. Others suffered similar fates to the first men to be dealt death by these spears, blood, limbs, and body parts thrown everywhere as the blades bit home.

Jarl Bjorn and the two men on either side all had their lives ended as three blades slammed home in unison, Jarl Bjorn was shouting his defiance, and the blade went into his open mouth and crashed out the other side of his head his son was stood behind him as his father's blood and shards of skull showered his face. Healfden wailed "FATHER" as he dropped dead at his son's feet, the two warriors whose duty was to protect their Jarl died also with the spears punching through the eye and skull of one and the other through his stomach due to his immense size and the stench of open bowels added to the metallic tang of blood.

CEOAL WAS PLEASED with the result and the devastation they had dealt the attackers. Healfden moved to attack the line, but men grabbed him pulling him away, two more grabbed the body of Jarl Bjorn, and the raiders melted from the front line of the shield wall and moved to withdraw Lavos saw all this and ran to help remove Healfden through the open southern gate, he knew the attackers had failed and needed to escape. Other men of Powys and Mercia noticed the devastating attack and looked at the carnage the spears had wrecked on the battle brothers, and they too edged away. The raiders nearly fell out of the gate struggling with the burden of the dead Jarl and the howling frustrated Healfden.

OSWI LOOKED at his men they were battle-worn, blood-splattered gaps had appeared, and he could see that half of his guard of Farndon was down either dead already or dying from some vicious wound. Bern spoke "We need to expel them and close the gate sir" Oswi nodded he knew they might lose more men, but Bern as ever was correct the attackers needed to be evicted from Farndon, and if they could kill more then so much the better as they may not then try to attack again.

Bern hefted his shield and sword and shouted "Prepare" The line adjusted and all raised shields and swords to be ready for the next commands, all were aching, cut, battered, and exhausted but they would not falter now when Thane Oswi and Farndon needed them.

Bern spoke again "STEP FORWARD" As one of the line stepped over the mound of dead towards the retreating enemy, panic appeared on the faces of some who quickly turned scrambling for the gate pushing and shoving each other over to escape. Once more Bern spoke "STEP FORWARD" Each step took them closer to attacking the fleeing enemy, the group by the gate was melting into the darkness. Oswi could hear screams of men and noticed Eleen now directing spears and arrows to be launched over the wall as the men scrambled over the rocks looking to escape the death inside the walls of Farndon. A third time Bern spoke "STEP FORWARD" They were now nearly upon the gate, a few brave attackers darted forward slashing at shields to slow the men of Farndon down but to no avail like the tide of the sea the men flowed forward killing as they went. Soon no attacker was alive inside the gateway. Bern and Lan stepped forward and slammed the gate shut dropping the heavy locking bars in place.

Oswi turned and looked at the men "Men we have won this battle, well done we have no time to rest on the walls"

All the men responded moving to ladders to climb upon the wall.

CHAPTER 22
THE RETREAT

The guards, the King's troop, and the villagers of Farndon all ran like hounds of hell were chasing them up the ladders to the village walls.

The dead dying and wounded of Farndon and the attackers were left where they lay the men needed to reach the wall. Oswi, Bern, Lan, and Ceoal reached the wall first and stood looking down the rocky path, bodies lay strewn across the rocks where Eleen and the young and old of Farndon had peppered the retreating warriors with arrows and spears. Bern pointed to groups of the attackers huddled in the shelter of the rocks, others had reached the river, though they could not use the boats they had crossed from Holt with earlier.

ALFE and his men had been unable to stop the raiders from crossing the bridge the numbers had been too great and even though arrows and spears had thinned the attackers of the watchtower down the main group had passed the barricade and ran the gauntlet of fire to reach the bridge and safety. Jarl Bjorn had left a small rear guard at the Holt side of the bridge, but they had been dealt with when Alfe and his men slowly and quietly slipped down the side of the watch-tower using the dark the crawled through the undergrowth towards the waiting group of warriors.

ONCE CLOSE ENOUGH TO quickly charge Alfe and his men stood throwing their remaining spears at the small group. Alfe had shouted and ran as his men launched the spears he saw half of the group hit blood spraying the road and walls of the bridge the dead and dying falling into the river and other warriors. The leader growled his defence snatching his axe and spear he ran straight at Alfe. Alfe was swift and agile he reached the leader before his men had even set off, he slid across the shingle of the road dropping to a small crouch as the leader attacked Alfe slid between the man's legs as he ran towards him slicing his seax up into the man's groin blood splashed over Alfe's face as the leader staggered and fell blood gushing from this slashed groin he staggered a few steps before falling down dead.

Alfe sprang to his feet as his men joined him, they ran shouting and screaming at the warriors slicing, stabbing, kicking punching it was a gutter fight, knives, and seax slashed shields slammed into chests and faces, Alfe's men tore into the attackers like frenzied dogs the fight was quick and brutal in the end all the men who had been left to defend the bridge were dead.

ALFE STOOD his chest heaving from the fight. He turned and looked around his men, he was saddened by what he saw from his section he had lost six men he now stood with his remaining four they all carried cuts and bruises, but all smiled at Alfe they had won through. Alfe ached he had never fought as hard before he looked to the village where he could see the attackers still climbing the rocks to reach the open southern gate. Alfe noticed one of his men leaning over the wall of the bridge he turned to Alfe "Alfe should we head over the bridge and burn those boats the scum arrived on" Alfe stepped over and the remaining men followed they all looked at the scattered small boats at the bottom of the far side of the bridge. Alfe laughed "Shall we?" the men smiled and as one they set off running over the bridge to cause mischief. They ran over the bridge racing each other and giggling like young maids.

THEY SOON REACHED the far side and scrambled down the side of the bridge they used caution now as they were unsure if any guards had been left. Reaching the river bank, they looked at the cluster of boats, Alfe turned to see one of his men still negotiating the climb down he had a lit firebrand in his hand. Alfe smiled in his haste he had forgotten that. The men scrambled about smashing planks and throwing shrubs wicker baskets from the men who fished the river into the boats before setting light to them. Alfe also instructed the men to then push the boats back into the river. The boats would not be usable now, he motioned to his men, and they scrambled back up to the bridge and watched as the flames consumed the small boats floating in the river.

HE LOOKED up to the walls of Farndon he could hear the clash of weapons and the thud of shield on shield, the screams of pain as men slashed, stabbed, and cut at each other.

The men stood leaning on the bridge they had fought hard and well, but the night was not yet over, Alfe walked up the track towards Farndon, he could see the small hand carts that the merchants used to transport goods from the river to Farndon and beyond. Alfe looked back to the bridge and grabbing a cart pulled it down to the open entrance of the bridge. His remaining men watched him as he dragged the cart down and tipped it onto its side to start forming a barrier. He turned and looked at his men, "We need to block the bridge Thane Oswi will not want the scum to escape across the river." With that, he walked back up the track for another cart.

THE MEN LOOKED at each other and dutifully followed Alfe up the track all dragging carts down to stack them against each other. They could hear the battle continuing inside the walls of Farndon, they had moved six carts to block the access to the river, and they found a large tree trunk which they hauled up from the river to fasten ropes around making the barricade of carts stronger. Alfe sent two men across the bridge to pilfer shields from the dead attackers these too were attached to the carts. Alfe listened to the battle he heard some strange new commands "HOLD, THRUST" carry down to where he and his men worked hard at the bridge. The screams of pure agony floated down to them all the men stopped but could hear Ceoal and Oswi shouting again. Alfe spoke to his men "Quickly go grab as many spears and spare swords as you can. I think the battle has just turned in our favor, we need to be ready"

THE MEN RUSHED to obey as the crash of weapons continued. The shouts and screams of pain still filtered down as Alfe stood alone at the barricade. His men soon returned with bundles of spears and swords, at least they had plenty of weapons. Alfe stood on the crumbling wall of the bridge watching as a trickle of men started to retreat from the southern gateway, the trickle soon became a flood of men as the survivors of the pitched battle within the confines of Farndon ran for their lives. Alfe could see people on the southern wall shooting arrows and throwing spears into the warriors as they clambered down the steep rocky paths to escape the nightmare of the failed attack. "Men stand ready, we must deny them access to the bridge" His tired worn men grimly pulled belts tight hefted spears and stood ready to repel any who ventured to the bridge. Alfe watched as men scrambled over the rocks to escape the barrage of missiles thrown at the attackers as they fled the confines of Farndon, he saw the light from the gate disappear as it was slammed shut.

The enemy had been evicted from Farndon. Alfe and his men watched as the would-be attackers now hid in the rocks to escape the arrows and spears from the walls of Farndon. Small groups of men braved the hail of missiles to try and reach the river. The surprise they received on reaching the river was not a pleasant one. They stood shock on their faces as they noticed the burning remnants of boats floating down the river. Arguments and scuffles soon started between the men who had been allied to attack Farndon.

Alfe and his men stood atop the bridge safe behind the barrier of logs, ropes, and carts watching them and laughing. They noticed a larger second group nearing the bottom of the rock pathway all these men were better armed and carried the same shield with a black crow on it. They carried a body between them, one man was visibly dragged away screaming and cursing as he looked up at Farndon to where Oswi stood. Alfe could see Oswi, Bern, and Ceoal all stood on top of the wall watching as the men struggled to retreat to safety away from the walls of Farndon. It was Ceoal with his keen eyesight that first saw the boats or what was left of them smouldering as they bobbed along the slow-moving river. He pointed to them surprised by the sight Oswi and Bern looked confused it was Lan who realised who was responsible "Alfe" was all he uttered. Bern started laughing "Look on the bridge is that him?" they all turned staring in amazement at the crude barrier across the access to the bridge it was Ceoal who responded, "Yes, I am sure that is Alfe, he has not many men left with him but look on the bridge they have made a good account of themselves so far."

Oswi and the others watched as the attackers climbed back up from the river bank to join with the group of raiders who had also escaped from Farndon.

THE GROUP WAS STILL large and could cause a problem if it wished to, but most of these men were now seeking to escape from the battle and did not wish to die. They trudged along the path towards the bridge, as Alfe had predicted they looked to cross the river and reach safety. It did not take long for the men to arrive at the track that led from the bridge. They stood looking and pointing shouting at each other as they saw the barricade. Retreat was proving harder than the battle they had just encountered within Farndon. The attackers had come confident that they would break through across the river and bridge into the very village of Farndon and make havoc, killing, raping, and stealing, they had seen Farndon as an easy target. Now more than half of them lay dead and many more were wounded either trapped within Farndon or bleeding, dying along the path through the rocks.

OSWI WATCHED as the raiders of the now-dead Jarl Bjorn joined with the remnants of the Mercian traitors and men of Powy's. They still numbered around forty to fifty men which could still cause havoc should they wish to. Aruth appeared on the wall walking slowly he had been strapped with bandages and replaced his armour to join the men on the wall

Oswi spoke with him, "Are you sure you need to be here" Aruth smiled "I am your appointed captain my remaining men are still in the fight though I am sorry to say I think we lost half of them in the assault on the gateway, the scum that attacked us did not die easily."

Oswi nodded "I am afraid that Alfe has lost most of his section too and he has blocked the attacker's retreat, I feel that they have bitten off more than they can chew, come look" Oswi helped Aruth along the wall to stand with Bern, Ceoal, and Lan. Aruth leaned on the wall for support and looked down to the river and bridge, "Oh, Alfe, you have done well but I feel you have cornered an angry bear"

Bern spoke, "They could be okay, they will be hard to reach across the barricade and the scum seem to have lost the will to fight, they may just try to escape further downriver."

Ceoal was still watching the enemy as they jostled each other, checking shields and weapons, and forming lines, he noticed the raiders had taken command of the makeshift group of warriors and were encouraging them to fight once more, he turned to inform Oswi but noticed all his comrades were now looking at the small brave band stood by the barricade, Alfe and his men could not hope to hold it for long as they must have been outnumbered by nearly ten to one. The odds were definitely not in their favour.

OSWI VISIBLY SHOOK, he hoped that Alfe and whoever remained behind the barricade would run and hide, they could not hope to defeat or even stop the rampaging tide of the attackers that stood before them, they would all be killed as the warriors swamped over the defences to escape, these were desperate men. Bern looked at Oswi, he could see the pain in the young man's face he had already lost a lot of men under his command this night, and yes more of the enemy had been killed than men of Farndon but he knew Oswi well and he would be blaming himself and now he stood safe on a wall looking where a small defiant band of his household guards prepared to do battle which would ultimately lead to their deaths. Bern reached out and touched Oswi on the shoulder "Do not fear for the men with Alfe, they have chosen their destiny this night, they are warriors we should be proud of." Oswi looked at his old mentor "I am proud of them Bern, I wish I was with them" The group stood watching on the wall it was too late now any action they took would mean more deaths to Farndon and Alfe and his band would still be defeated, the die had been cast.

CHAPTER 23
THE SLAUGHTER

Alfe looked over the barricade at the group of warriors stood looking towards him, he felt they were all looking directly at him. The raiders had organised the remnants of the groups into a single unit all checked straps and weapons, hefted shields as they prepared. Alfe looked at his men they too had seen what was happening and they knew they could not hold the barricade for long the sheer weight of numbers of the men stood jostling each other as they organised their lines would mean they only needed one strong attack to wipe them out. Alfe climbed and stood on the large truck looking down at his men.

"Men, I can ask no more of you today, you have all served with me today and defiantly risked all for our loved ones and Farndon, We do have not the numbers to hold back the horde we now face and our comrades in Farndon will not reach us in time, I will stand here at the barricade I will try my best to keep the attacking scum busy while you all go over the bridge and hide take your chances to split up, go now my brothers and thank you" Alfe turned and garbed a handful of spears propping them against the barricade.

• • •

THE MEN TURNED they had been directed to leave they slowly walked away. One man stopped and looked at his fellows, the rest all looked and by some unspoken word, they all nodded and turned back. They too grabbed spears and climbed upon the log to stand with their leader and comrade in one final action and act of total defiance to the scum who had invaded their land, their village. They would not run and hide they would kill as many as they could and stand tall together friends in life and friends in death. Alfe felt the barricade creak as each man stepped up, he knew no words to describe the joy, terror, brotherhood, respect, and fear he had for these men, they would all die here today at this barricade across the river selling their lives dearly. A single tear came to Alfe's eye he was so proud of them, he need not say more they had all decided their own fate. They would walk the realms of the afterlife together.

Oswi, Bern, Ceoal, Lan, and Aruth along with the King's troop and surviving men of the guards of Farndon all saw Alfe, and his small band step up to the barricade to stand ready and give battle to the retreating horde of attackers. Aruth looked sad, as he knew these men would all be killed that day, such bravery. Oswi looked at his face ashen the agony was etched on his young face as he saw the loyalty of these men. Death would be the end here today.

HEALFDEN WAS STILL furious at the death of his father, he cajoled, shouted, pushed, and shoved his men into line. He was soon shouting at Lavos and his few men along with a man who led the scum from Powy's it took time, but he had them all ready for action four lines drawn up to attack the barricade and then escape. Healfden would return to seek vengeance on Farndon. He would burn Farndon to the ground for the death of his father, Healfden needed to get his father's men away, they had lost too many men today. He encouraged the men to step out in their lines to reach the blocked bridge. He could see the small band of men atop the barricade with spears held ready, looking around he anticipated the first line would all die upon the spears maybe a few from the second as they slaughtered the few men stood defiantly blocking the route to safety. Idiots he thought what did they truly think would happen to them, they should have run and hidden after burning the boats. Slowly the lines of men inched forward towards the barricade they shouted and chanted to encourage each other. Healfden looked at the barricade as the men drew closer and closer, the defenders were a good head taller than his men and would have the advantage when using the spears, he spoke to his own men and advised them to work in pairs one to get the attention of the defenders whilst the other would try to kill them.

Oswi and the others continued to watch the horde of warriors step closer and closer to Alfe, his men and the barricade. Oswi was deeply upset even if he and all the men that they had left mounted horses they would not reach them in time to save Alfe and they ran the risk of all ending up dead. Leaving Farndon open to further attacks. The men along the wall tried to throw spears and shoot arrows, but the distance was too great, spears bounced off rocks any arrow that reached the attackers had no power left to it and bounced off the track or off the coats and mail of the attackers. Alfe was doomed they would soon be overwhelmed and slaughtered, Oswi wished he could turn away, but in some macabre nightmare, he continued as everyone else did to watch the events play out.

At the barricade, Alfe and his few men stood ready, spears close to hand shields strapped to their backs for protection if anyone got close to swing an axe or sword over their heads as they tried to spear the attackers. He could see Alfe on the wall and raised a spear high in the air as a salute to his Thane, Alfe had enjoyed his life Oswi had been fair and pushed his men hard, but all loved him and would give up their lives for him as they did now, Alfe knew that Oswi would look after his wife and newborn son they would be kept safe within Farndon. He looked to his men "Stand ready men" They all stepped up grim-faced and looked death in its face as it stormed towards them like a horned dark beast on a black crazed horse.

CEOAL HAD MOMENTARILY LEFT the wall, and he ran back pushing between Bern and Oswi, he spoke frantically "Has anyone seen Raffe" Oswi looked around the wall and pondered if he was honest he had not seen him during the night, he looked to Bern, "Did he not go with you to help get everyone from Crag Rock?" Bern himself looked confused "Yes he did, and I saw him back within the confines of Farndon once we had everyone inside"

Oswi paced the wall, he kept looking over at Alfe and the warriors creeping slowly forward, but where was Raffe. It would have to wait, he just hoped he was safe he was a distant cousin and he had been left in his care as a squire.

A hand touched his shoulder Oswi turned to see the warriors were a step from the barricade he saw Alfe, and his men stood poised ready to repel them.

OSWI SAW Alfe pointing with his spear to the hills inland he faintly heard his name being called by Eleen "Oswi, Oswi, The King has arrived" Oswi looked back to Alfe and the attackers who had now stopped. They too must have been wondering what Alfe was pointing at. Oswi quickly ran to the North wall and stood on the tower over the gate looking to the hills, he was astonished at the sight his eyes gave him. Eleen was correct though still some distance Oswi could see his King and other Lord's Banners flying in the wind as they raced down the valley towards Farndon.

. . .

Bern had been correct, Raffe had returned with him from Crag Rock helping to ensure that all of the people safely reached Farndon. The Northern gate was still open as people from the outlying settlements had not yet reached Farndon. Raffe had climbed down from his horse leading her to the stables when Lady Eleen had caught up with him.

"Raffe, I need you to leave Farndon," She spoke quickly "Come take your saddle and take my horse, he is strong and rested" Raffe followed Lady Eleen he did not wish to say no to her, "My lady I must stay here with the others, they will have need of me" Eleen smiled sweetly at the young Raffe "Hush now, I have spoken with Thane Oswi and he has agreed this everyone is busy so I offered to assist you and give you Oswi's message" Raffe saw no reason to doubt the truth of it, why would he. Lady Ellen deftly assisted him with saddling her horse, Raffe was soon astride it with a small bag with food and drink and another of oats and hay for the horse, Eleen passed Raffe a spear and his sword. "Listen Raffe, the King has been out searching for the raiders last Thane Oswi heard he was around two days North of Farndon, and we believe he was heading back this way Oswi has tasked you to find him explain we are surrounded and ask the King if he can come to our aid" all the time she held Raffe's hands looking directly into his eyes as she relayed the message. Eleen walked him to the gate and saw him leave and race North. Eleen hated lying to the young squire Oswi knew nothing of what she had just undertaken she only hoped Raffe would find the King and return with him in time to help save Farndon. Raffe had ridden fast Lady Eleen's horse was sleek, and sure-footed, he raced along the hills and fields as if his very world was crumbling behind him. Raffe had done well, in less than half a day's ride he found the King and a host of Lords with him. Raffe was lucky his great uncle Ealdorman Ludeca was still with the King after recovering from his wounds, he was soon in the King's tent passing on the message from Thane Oswi.

. . .

THE NEXT MORNING the King rode hard to reach Farndon, he took with him one hundred mounted warriors and Lords and the faithful Raffe to guide them. The King left his foot warriors behind and advised they marched to meet him as quickly as they could. The king sat astride his horse and looked down on Farndon, he was relieved to see Oswi's flag still flew, it was young Raffe who spotted the attackers forming to assault the barricaded bridge. The King hurriedly spoke with his Lords and the hundred horses thundered down the hillside with a hundred hard faced experienced warriors screaming and shouting for joy, spears, swords, shields, and axes all held ready to take slaughter upon the raiders who dared to keep invading their beloved Mercia. The ground shook, turf flew as the horses galloped mail and weapons clashed the noise of the King and his warriors became louder and louder as they headed to save Farndon and her people.

ALFE STOOD high on the barricade his fist pumping the spear up and down in the air as he laughed loudly, they were safe he and his men the King had arrived how, why, he didn't care. The men with Alfe joined in laughing and shouting clasping arms of each other and slapping each other's backs they would live to fight another day. Oswi, watched as the King approached the timely arrival meant that Alfe and his men were safe, but how did the King know, he looked around and felt Eleen at his side as she gently touched his hand, "Oswi my Thane" she said quietly and courteously Oswi looked her in the eyes "Eleen,?" she lowered her head "I confess, I instructed Raffe to leave Farndon and seek the Kings help, do not chastise him as I lied and told him I was acting on your instructions, forgive me" Oswi smiled and gently lifted her face to look at her "Oh Eleen, there is nothing to forgive, you acted in good faith and thought of something we men did not" Oswi leaned down and gently kissed Eleen's cheek she blushed and once more hid her face standing close to Oswi as her heart was soaring.

THE BETRAYAL

. . .

THE KING and his loyal Lords thundered onto the wide track around the Northern wall and gate, the horde of attackers stood pointing panic washed over them like rain from the sky, disorder, and escape were on each person's mind. A few brave souls stood hankered down behind shields to face the oncoming onslaught others ran to the towards the walls of Farndon, others towards the fields and Crag Rock, some stripped off mail and weapons and braved the icy river to cross to safety. Healfden and his loyal men ran down the small path of the river Orm remembered that small boats were sometimes anchored at the pier near Crag Rock, and this opened up a possible escape route for them.

THE ATTACKING warriors panicked and tried to hide but to no avail one hundred angry warriors astride one hundred trained warhorses hit them hard. The impact of the horses threw bodies into the air, others fell as they ran to be trampled by heavy hooves which crushed skulls and smashed bones. Others had spears rammed through their bodies, some had axes or swords driven into heads and shoulders either crushing skulls to splatter blood and gore over the attacking horses or slicing deep into shoulders and chests the impact so hard they died before they fell. Once the King's men had rampaged through the main body of attackers they dispersed into smaller groups to seek out the scum who hid, the King had been strict with his orders "KILL THEM ALL" he had shouted, and his men obeyed. Oswi watched as the attackers were slaughtered by the barricade once the King's warriors had passed by to seek out the isolated men retreating he could see the havoc they had created with bodies crushed, limbs missing the track was covered with blood and gore it looked like some wild monster had lain waste to the area. Oswi turned to his men at the gate "Open the gate our King has arrived" Oswi climbed down from the wall as he had seen the King along with the absent Raffe turn and head up the track to Farndon with his father and the Kings Guard.

CHAPTER 24
THE CHASE

Oswi stood with Bern and Eleen in the courtyard as King Offa and his father arrived with the missing squire Raffe. All three bowed their heads as the King climbed down from his war horse which still looked like it could race on for the rest of the day.

"Lord King, Thank you," Oswi said as the King approached. The King laughed I think I should be thanking you Oswi, it looks like you have been busy trapping those scum, we managed to almost wipe them out, we chased a large warband some days ago when they attacked further North. It seems you have found me another group to do battle with." "Yes King Offa, though this group has Jarl Bjorn's men along with some from Powy's and your old friend Sigmund and Lavos" laughed Oswi. The King slapped Oswi hard on the back "You seem to attract danger and enemies young Oswi, come show me what you did." Oswi started to walk off with the King who stopped as a warrior raced into the open gateway. It was Harrick Captain of the Kings Guard.

. . .

"KING OFFA, the men are checking everywhere to make sure there are no stragglers, we have found the body of Jarl Bjorn laid out on the river footpath that leads to Crag Rock, at least a dozen or more footprints go that way" It was Oswi that spoke next "We killed Bjorn within the walls and his son Healfden, and remaining warriors carried his body out, they know the area and will be aware some fishermen leave boats at the small pier at Crag Rock, they mean to escape"

The King kicked at the ground frustration on his face, "Harrick call in my personal guard we will give chase immediately, Oswi grab yourself a horse, I am sure you will enjoy the chase"

Oswi quickly jumped onto a horse that a warrior offered and turned to follow Harrick and his King out of the Northern gateway and down the track to the bridge as they rode Harrick was shouting out names of the King's personal guard he could see and soon had a troop of around twenty men once more thundering after their King, whooping with joy.

HEALFDEN and his men saw King Offa and his rampaging horsemen and knew the battle of Farndon was lost. He looked at the torn body of his father, it did not sit well with him, but he knew he must leave him here at the river or they would not escape. Orm his father's steersman advised that if they went back to the old pier down the river they might find a few small boats to escape in or also further down the river was shallower and a man could walk the width of the river though the water would reach most men's chest and faces. It was the only option they had if they wished to survive. Healfden could not believe that the village had been so strong in its defence, even though they had penetrated the wall the men had been trained well and withstood all the attacks from his father's warriors, the Welsh and the Mercian's, he would check with that idiot Lavos as to who led the people and warriors at Farndon it had all gone wrong, Healfden had advised his father not to trust Lavos and the turd

Sigmund, and he had paid the ultimate price. Orm led them down an overgrown path that followed the river towards Crag Rock they had not gone far when he heard shouts and horses moving quickly again, they had been spotted, he ran faster to catch Orm, and the men followed none wished to be killed now when escape was within their grasps.

HARRICK LED the way with Raffe in single file down the small path alongside the river followed by a few of the King's Guard then Oswi and the King. The King was laughing and shouting as if he was giving chase to a fox or a boar out hunting. Oswi had learned that the raiders could be as wily as any fox and as stubborn and deadly as any wild boar. The King was determined they should chase these men down. They could not ride as fast along the path as it was narrow for a charging horse. The small group of enemy stood along the pier desperately trying to board two small fishing boats. The boats were not big enough for all the men as a few others had followed Healfden. Healfden had made sure he got all his remaining warriors on the boats. He laughed as they pushed the boats into the slow-moving river. He stood watching the panic on the faces of the men left behind.

The disposed Lord Sigmund and two of his warriors and the idiot Lavos with his one remaining warrior. Healfden shouted to them. "Try and swim across" laughing loudly. Sigmund stood cursing. He turned as he could hear the shouts and chants and thrum of the horse's hooves on the hard-packed ground.

SIGMUND LOOKED at Lavos "In the shit now, come we move, the river I understand is passable further upstream we have no time to waste"

Sigmund ran jumping off the pier to sprint along the path once more. His two loyal men threw down their shields and set off after him, without the shields they could move faster. Lavos grunted and looked to Cernwulf "Let us move fast, we will receive no mercy from the King, Lavos threw down his shield keeping hold of his spear and sword he may still have need of them. They ran down the track after Sigmund. Harrick, Raffe, and the leading men arrived at the pier, the leading warriors ran down the pier and launched their small spears into the air at Healfden and the small boats, the spears fell short. Harrick could hear the men in the boats laughing. King Offa and Oswi arrived with more men some had bows and arrows. King Offa looked at the boats "It is the raider scum, you men try and reach them with your arrows" The three men jumped down quickly to respond standing at the far point of the pier they shot arrow after arrow into the air, and the raiders still laughed at the King's men. One raider stood baring his arse to the King and shouting insult after insult. Harrick marched down the pier anger on his face he held out his arm to the nearest warrior "Your bow now" Harrick had been brought up to use a bow and arrow as fast as he could walk he carried one, his father had been an excellent warrior and tasked Harrick and his brothers hard. Harrick aimed sighting the arrow turning slightly out of the direct wind he pulled the shaft back then grunted and pulled it back further the wood of the bow creaked in pain the string was taught, and neither would move no further back, Harrick calmly looked at his target and breathed slowly "Got you arsehole, you will not insult my King again" everyone including the King was watching Harrick as he let out his breath and the arrow shot with immense power from the bow with a loud twang.

 The laughing warrior who still had his arse out half stood turning his head to shout more insults, Harrick's arrow took the warrior straight through the open mouth smashing his teeth and coming out the back of his head, his body shook and fell into the river. The other raiders went quiet and watched the body floating blood mixing with the water. Healfden looked at Orm who shrugged "Some shot" With that they sailed away now safe as they neared the far bank and the river bend. They had survived and would live to fight again. Healfden looked across the river to see Oswi and King

Offa looking at him. With a deep hatred deep inside him, Healfden blamed them for his father's death. He drew his seax and sliced his palm dripping blood into the river as he shouted at them "I swear I will seek my revenge on you, I will be hidden in the shadows watching, waiting, we will have your soul Lord of Farndon you and any loved ones will not be safe from Jarl Healfden of the Black Crows" his men cheered him and with one last look as the boat rounded the bend in the river.

King Offa looked at Oswi and smiled "Well Oswi, seems you have a lifelong enemy to deal with" Oswi smiled "Maybe Harrick should have shot the new Jarl Healfden, my Lord King" King Offa laughed at Oswi's reply. Harrick strode back down the pier to his King smiling "I enjoyed that, the little shit was annoying me" Harrick stopped and looked around "Where is young Raffe my Lord" Oswi snapped his head around as did King Offa "Look there" shouted King Offa, "He is chasing someone further along the river path." Oswi looked hard at the young squire shouting and riding hard after two men he grimaced "Lavos and Cernwulf" Harrick quickly mounted his horse "Young idiot he will be no match for those two" With that he galloped after Raffe. Oswi followed as did King Offa and his men. They raced after Raffe as fast as they could. Oswi noticed a flash of armour a short distance in front of Lavos he looked again as the three running men broke cover of some large shrubs turning to King Offa as they raced on "Sigmund, is further in front Lord King" King Offa looked down the path and shouted loud "Sigmund the Snake, come feel my blade" Sigmund half turned seeing his King chase him down, Sigmund felt a cold chill run down his spine..

Raffe had not stayed to watch Captain Harrick shoot his bow, he had seen Lavos and gave chase, young Raffe was besotted with Lady Eleen, and seeing Lavos running the path had angered the young squire resulting with the action and chase. Faster he went he was determined to catch them. Lavos had seen the lone horseman give chase. Cernwulf was slowing down he was not as young as he used to be and could not keep pace with Lavos he cursed and looked back to see the horseman on top of him, he had nowhere to move, he could feel the breath of the horse at his neck he pulled his sword to turn and swing at the horseman, he was too slow, Raffe kicked the horse to speed up and swung his sword into the neck of Cernwulf as he quickly rode past him. Raffe was giddy, he had done it he had killed, and he would kill again Lavos would feel his blade. Cernwulf dropped spluttering as blood pumped from his ruptured neck he tumbled down the grass slope his body half falling into the river.

Lavos ran on Sigmund had nearly reached the river crossing now, he had seen Cernwulf killed and noticed that it was one of the young squires who chased them down. Lavos laughed he would deal with the boy squire now. Lavos spun quickly spear in his meaty right hand, he stood leaned back, and launched the spear as Raffe neared him moving so fast he did not have time to react, as the spear flew true and straight taking young Raffe straight through the chest the force of the throw dragged him clean off the horse to fall dead on the pathway.

Harrick and Oswi could plainly see Lavos as he stopped and turned Oswi shouted "NO," but it was no good the spear flew true and snatched Raffe's life away. Harrick charged on Oswi and shouted to him "Harrick Sigmund he is near the crossing" Harrick nodded "He is mine" Oswi knew Harrick would not stop until Sigmund was dead or captured. This left Oswi to deal with Lavos, something Oswi was going to enjoy. Lavos had turned from the river and was running inland, he knew there were ditches and small stream beds he could hide in and hopefully not be found. Oswi turned and chased after him soon covering the ground as the horse could move easier than on the narrow path Harrick and three guards rushed to the river's edge to catch Sigmund. King Offa pulled up looking around seeing Oswi was alone he and a few guards quickly followed him he pointed to the river for the remaining guards who quickly followed their Captain.

Oswi was seething inside, Raffe was a hard-working young man and faithful he did not deserve what fate had handed him. Closer and closer Oswi was gaining ground fast he would soon reach Lavos he pushed the horse faster and faster. Lavos was starting to panic he would not reach the stream bed, he glanced over his shoulder to see how many men followed him, he was instantly enraged when he saw the lone figure of Oswi. Lavos skidded to a halt in the long grass pulling his sword from its strap over his shoulder he half-turned swinging the sword. Oswi pulled the reins to steer the horse past Lavos, but he was too late the heavy blade bit into the right shoulder of the fast-moving horse cutting deep and smashing the bone, the horse collapsed sliding along the floor, Oswi was launched out of the saddle to land in a heap. Lavos moved over the ground fast towards Oswi luckily Oswi recovered in time and was on his feet sword in hand. Lavos wasted no time and swung the sword at Oswi's head who ducked quickly following up with a thrust to the chest of Lavos which he knocked aside to swing and slice at Oswi's leg. Oswi managed to sidestep the attack and back swung his sword to slice into his arm of Lavos. The cut was only shallow but enraged Lavos even more he swung again and again at Oswi with no respite attacks came fast to his head, chest, legs, and arms Oswi was stepping back with each attack though defending well as none had struck home. Oswi jumped backward leaving a bigger gap between Lavos and him so that Lavos last attack flew through thin air then Oswi rushed in kicking Lavos in the chest and smashing the pommel of his sword into his face. Lavos was stunned and Oswi continued slashing at Lavos hitting home on his arms and chest, Lavos was struggling he was short of breath from the kick to his chest and half blinded from his smashed nose and face. Oswi continued to attack and thrust, Lavos defended but Oswi struck home slicing Lavos more and more. Lavos was now retreating stepping backwards he stumbled on a rock arms spinning he lost his grip on his sword which flew from his hand to land in the long grass.

Lavos was soon flat out on the grass, Oswi was stood over him now with his sword point touching his throat, his hands were shaking such was his fury, and anger. Lavos eyes were wide with fear he could see the madness of battle in Oswi "NO, Please NO" he uttered. Oswi did not care Lavos was going to die, he slowly leaned on his sword a gloved hand reached for the blade, and a calm voice spoke to him "Oswi, NO, we will take him back to Farndon, do not kill him this way you will regret it" Oswi's body shook from the adrenaline he turned and looked into the face of his King and stepped back from Lavos. The King's men quickly tied Lavos up and dragged him off.

King Offa looked at Oswi "Come, my young noble warrior, we must see how Harrick and the men fared." With that, the King climbed onto his horse and reached his hand down for Oswi who swung up behind his King and they trotted back to the river to find Harrick and the others. The King tasked further troops to care for the dead Raffe who had been killed by Lavos.

HARRICK and his two warriors had arrived at the river's edge to see the ex-Ealdorman Sigmund and his own remaining two warriors waist-deep at the river crossing. Harrick looked at his two men "We make the horses charge into the river, we should then catch them, and have the advantage of height over them, are you ready?" Both warriors drew swords and nodded at their captain, "CHARGE" shouted Harrick and kicked his own horse to splash into the flowing river, his men quickly followed, and the three horses jumped through the water spraying water everywhere. The last in the line of Sigmund's warriors turned hearing the splashing charging warriors, panicking he threw off his weapons and turned holding his arms outstretched, Harrick and his men were already on top of him, and he disappeared under the water as the horses hit him, the river turned red as hooves smashed his head and chest, he died quickly as the icy water filled his lungs. Harrick and his men charged on. Sigmund and his last warrior were nearly across the river, they crashed on through the water to escape the horses and men of the King's troop icy fear gripped Sigmund he had gambled and failed. They reached the far bank of the river trying to climb out up the muddy bank and failing. Sigmund stopped when he heard and felt the hot, snorting breath at his neck from Harrick's horse. He turned looking at the grim face of Harrick "Surrender, Sigmund."

King Offa arrived back at the river Lavos was now on his way back to Farndon as a prisoner, he and Oswi watched as Sigmund roped to the Saddle of Harrick was dragged back through the river to his King.

The fight for Farndon was over, the disloyal ex-captain of Farndon was now a prisoner of the King as was the disposed Ealdorman Sigmund. They would both sit in judgment of the King and their peers.

CHAPTER 25
THE AFTERMATH

The King, Thane Oswi, and Harrick returned victorious with their prisoners to Farndon. Rolf and his assistant Fulk along with Lady Eleen and Goodwife Frey were all busy tending to the wounded. Wives and children of Farndon's dead guards and warriors sat sobbing some having found husbands had pulled the bodies from the carnage at the southern gate. Brak and the men of the village were segregating the men of Farndon from the abundance of dead raiders, Mercian, and men of Powy's these now dragged outside the walls here groups of men who had helped build the walls, slowly piled the dead, and stacked timbers, dried grasses and soaked the whole stack in oils so they could burn them all on a funeral pyre.

BERN HAD ORGANISED the remaining men of Farndon and the King's troop he commanded into two groups to stand watch on the wall through the evening. Aruth had finally collapsed from his injured back and had been taken to his private hut to rest, Alfe had returned to Farndon with the three men left of his section. Lan was still busy

THE BETRAYAL

he had six men still. In the section that Drom had commanded only two men survived they had stood the whole battle within the village walls next to Oswi and Bern and sold their lives dearly after hearing of the betrayal of Drom their section leader both men stood vacant eyes like ghosts, they would be no good this evening. Wareson's section had been hit hard too. Wareson was wounded with a deep cut to his head he had only five of his section left alive who now stood on the wall with the others the guard of Farndon had started the previous night with a commander and four section leaders and forty guards. The village now had a wounded commander and section leader, leaving only two section leaders fit for duty, with only seventeen guards of which all had some minor wounds.

BERN HAD the men of the King's Troop under Ceoal moving the dead attackers from the rock path, these too would be added to the growing funeral pyre. Bern was surprised at how well the guards of Farndon had fought; he had seen how many had died from their bravery. The King's troops had suffered losses too at the end against the Jarl and his warriors they had killed men easily until Ceoal had launched the counterattack with the spears, a brilliant move. Ceoal now only had eight Kings troopers from his section of twelve, Bern had lost men too and only had five of his men left, he hoped the King would not be annoyed at losing eleven trained warriors they would be hard to replace. In total thirty-four men of Farndon had been killed. The only bonus that Bern had to offer was that the current count of the attackers was easily triple that.

KING OFFA SPOKE with Harrick and requested that he split the men who had raced with them to save Farndon into three groups two to stand watch and relieve the guards of Farndon to allow them to rest and attend to their fallen comrades. The third section is to assist with the disposal of the fallen attackers and clear the bridge including the barricades at each end. Harrick nodded in agreement he would ask for volunteers for the grisly task of dealing with the dead it would be no easy task.

King Offa walked around the compound talking to the wounded men and the children and wives of those killed, King Offa was deeply upset by the deaths and the anguish of the loved ones. He eventually made his way to Oswi's hall where Lady Eleen's maid Ethane had provided some hot food and ale, Eleen, Bern, Ceoal, and Oswi all stood as the King entered with Harrick and two guards who had stayed with the King all evening.

"Sit, sit do not stand on ceremony today my friends we should be grateful you all survived, and Farndon is still in Mercian hands"

Eleen put her hands to her face and started to sob, her body shook as the shock of the events finally hit her, Oswi leaned over and gently touched her shoulder she tried to smile but her face showed the pain, upset, and anguish to which she had succumbed. The King watched this and smiled he had pondered who he could match Eleen to her family had long supported the Kings of Mercia and a suitable noble needed to be found, now he had one.

King Offa sat at the table and Ethane passed him a bowl of potage and bread with some ale he smiled his thanks. They talked of the dead and wounded of Farndon the King though shocked remained composed as he was aware of how many of the attackers had been slain the village would survive and continue to grow because of the men like Ceoal, Bern, and their leader Oswi a great mind, excellent warrior he could be angered but also knew the strength of loyalty and compassion.

The King dismissed them all telling them to rest as he knew they all needed it he sat for a time with Harrick who had as Oswi suggested proved himself invaluable to the King, he was an excellent warrior, skilled with any weapon and loyal, and he worked his men hard to be better and stronger, Harrick was also a good tactician and was not afraid of suggesting to his King a different approach if he felt it was required. The King now spoke with Harrick.

"What do we do with our prisoners, my loyal captain" Harrick gulped more ale and looked at his King "They must die, and we must let people see it" The King frowned "What do you mean Harrick?" Harrick went on to explain that the King should send out riders to Thane's, Lords, Bishops, and other Clergy and leading men of Mercia to summon as many as he could here to Farndon so they could witness the death of Sigmund once an Ealdorman of King Offa and Lavos the former captain of Farndon. They must stand before the King and a man of God and answer to their betrayal and treachery. Then once they had confessed they should both be hung from scaffolds over the bridge so all could see and spread the word that death would be the only result of the betrayal of the King. King Offa listened to his captain and nodded his agreement to all. The King thanked him for his aid and left him to organise it all. It would take time for the leading people of Mercia to arrive and in that time, the scum got rot chained to posts in the middle of the yard of Farndon for all to see as they arrived. King Offa would ensure that his troops would assist with the repairs of Farndon, He also knew he must reward Oswi and his men for their stalwart defence of Farndon. He must speak with Oswi about the town over the river Holt he had heard it called.

DAYS WENT by Farndon slowly resembled its former look before the attack. The warriors and guards who had died defending Farndon had all been buried in a tomb together at the King's order they had died as brothers in arms and would sleep together as fallen brothers and warriors. Bern returned to Crag Rock with the families and his shrunken troop of guards. The King has said he would find replacements for him. Ceoal was in temporary command of the household guard of Farndon until Aruth was recovered. The clergy, Ealdorman, Lords, and Thane's all slowly arrived at Farndon it was soon a busy place as merchants and traders learned of all the visitors and arrived to ply their trade.

One morning King Offa arose and summoned Harrick to have a section of men ready and to ask Oswi and Eleen to be ready for a ride across the river. Harrick nodded and left; he was aware of what the King planned as he had visited the larger town of Holt across the river with him earlier in the week. Vern woke his master shaking him awake "Sir, Sir" Oswi stirred and looked at his young squire "Vern, what ails you?" asked Oswi after being shaken awake, "The King wishes for you to go out riding with him, you must get ready, I have arranged for yours and Lady Eleen's horses to be made ready." Oswi frowned "Lady Eleen? Is she aware?" enquired Oswi "Yes sir I woke her maid, she is helping Lady Eleen now, if you could get up and wash and dress I will quickly go and get some breakfast and a drink for you" with that Vern ran from Oswi's side to complete his tasks.

Oswi climbed out of bed quickly walking to the wooden desk and quickly washing in the warm water he grabbed an old shirt and dried himself down, Oswi was surprised at how attentive Vern was the water was fragranced with flowers and Oswi enjoyed that he smelt much fresher and cleaner. Oswi checked his clothes they were all freshly cleaned and also had a pleasant fragrance. He dressed quickly as Vern reappeared with some fresh warm bread and cheese that he had quickly grabbed from the baker. Oswi munched on the bread and cheese as Vern disappeared again to return with Oswi's freshly scrubbed chainmail and sword.

Oswi was soon ready and walking out into the courtyard towards the stable, His horse was stood ready as was Eleen's who appeared shortly after Oswi. The king's troops all stood waiting for the arrival of the King, Harrick walked across the courtyard towards Oswi smiling at him "The King will be here shortly, we are going for a ride across the river" King Offa appeared his mail polished to a high sheen smiling at Oswi and Eleen and nodding to Harrick "Are we all ready, Captain?" Harrick smiled "Yes Lord King, we are all here" Climbing onto his horse, he smiled at Oswi, and Eleen "Come my young friends, we shall have a ride out together." King Offa rode out with Harrick just behind him Oswi looked at Eleen and they both rode out and settled each side of the King as they rode through the gate and down the track towards the river. The King politely conversed with them as they slowly rode across the bridge and past the guarded watchtower which had recently had improvements and made taller and stronger. The bridge had had repairs too and was also now guarded. The King waved at the men and women working and returned the salute of the guards. All seemed calm in the area around Farndon the King was pleased.

CHAPTER 26
THE FUTURE

The King rode on talking with both Oswi and Eleen, they passed the road to Holt and ventured out to the fields where more folk toiled he pointed to small huts and barns out in the surrounding area. They soon reached a small wooden bridge over a stream which ran into the river Dee. A group of men were working on the bridge repairing it and strengthening it, guards stood at the far side. The King explained that the river and the bridge marked the boundary of his new land which he had taken control of after the death of the local Powy's leader Bledri who had attacked Farndon along with Jarl Bjorn, Sigmund, and Lavos.

THE KING TURNED his horse and motioned for Harrick to move away from them Harrick nodded and took two guards and slowly crossed the bridge to the other side of the river, the remaining guards moved a short distance from them. Oswi saw all this and was very surprised it was very rare that the King wished to speak in private to anyone let alone he and definitely not Eleen. The King slowly climbed from his horse letting it free to graze upon the lush grass instinctively Oswi

THE BETRAYAL

and Eleen followed suit. The King looked flustered and nervous as he walked a few steps away, turning he looked at Eleen first and walked towards her, Eleen startled stayed unmoving as the King reached out and took her tiny delicate hands in his big rough scared hands. "My dear I promised you on the death of your father I would take you as my ward and ensure you had a suitable marriage I have been remiss in my duties." Eleen looked down at her hands tenderly held by the King, the King continued "I have pondered long about this and my Lords have all put forward candidates for your hand" He laughed suddenly "I confess some I would not marry to a dead dog they are so bad" Eleen giggled at this herself, the King smiled and sighed as he spoke again "The problem I have is that the lords think you should marry someone of a higher station, a Lord, Ealdorman or possibly the eldest son of a Lord to ensure you are well looked after as a reward for your service to the crown." He once more went quiet released her hand and stepped back. Eleen bit her bottom lip nervously she did not wish to marry for power or privilege but for love, the King believed he was doing the right thing for her, how could she tell him what her heart desired? The King now looked to Oswi and spoke "My young loyal warrior, you have dealt with so much death and destruction and still have years to offer in service, you have already been rewarded by me and given land and title I know your heart's desire, but the Lords say you are not of a ranking Lord." He looked across the river, quiet once more. He kicked at a stone and turned to them both. "Am I not King of all Mercia, should I not decide what is for the best for my people?" Both Eleen and Oswi startled did not answer the King. "HARRICK" the King shouted and waved for him to re-join them. Oswi and Eleen looked at each other both utterly puzzled at the strange conversation with the King. Once Harrick and the guards had assembled by the King he spoke to Harrick "We ride to Holt I will address my Lords and Clergy, I have two items that need addressing now." Harrick led the way followed by the King with Oswi and Eleen in tow Eleen whispered to Oswi "Did you understand what was happening then?" Oswi shook his head he did not wish to voice his opinion he had dared to hope the King was giving Eleen to be his but was now so unsure.

The group made quick time across the small tracks through the fields. They soon arrived at Holt to find troops on gate duty and the Lords of Mercia sat talking in groups around the large open square in the centre of Holt. Oswi was surprised, Holt was at least double the size of Farndon and only had two walls that could be accessed from the land the other two stood atop sheer rock faces that dropped to the river below. Holt had more buildings, larger stables, and at the far end of the square stood an old stone Roman building, what its function had been Oswi was unsure but now it seemed this was the centre of power for Holt. The King jumped from his horse while it was still moving and strode across the open square a raised platform had been built at the far end and the King stomped up the steps to it and sat at a large high-backed chair. Harrick spoke with Oswi and Eleen, "Go stand near the front I have a feeling you will enjoy the King's anger." They both moved forward intrigued with the events unfolding before their eyes.

Harrick joined the King and spoke to a young man who ran to his bidding the King sat impatiently strumming his fingers in annoyance on the chair, eventually, two senior clergy appeared and sat on either side of their King. The Lords, Ealdorman, and Thanes of Mercia moved forward and stood looking up at the King waiting for him to speak. Harrick stepped towards the King after a quick hand signal, moments later under heavy guard two dirty, half-clothed, long-haired, and half-dressed men were pushed forward to stand in front of the King. Oswi spoke with Eleen "Lavos and Sigmund" Eleen gasped at the sight of these two once proud men.

The King nodded to Harrick once more.

"My Lord Bishops and Lords and people of Mercia, the King has called you all here to bring Sigmund and Lavos once a Lord and captain of the realm of Mercia to justice, you have all heard the information, what say you here and now?"

The assembled Lords all stood waiting for someone to speak. It was Ealdorman Alestan a lifelong friend to Oswi's father Ealdorman Ludeca. "DEATH" he shouted loudly, Oswi's father followed "DEATH" The shout echoed around all the Lords, Ealdorman, and Thanes shouting in agreement. The King looked to the two Bishops sitting on either side of him waiting patiently for their response it must be unanimous. The King sat unmoving the Bishops did not utter a response. Eleen looked at the lump of a man who had sworn to serve her father Lavos and walked towards him. The Bishops watched this young maid march over she grabbed a sword from a Lord as she quickened her pace. The King stood and spoke "Lady Eleen NO, we must serve justice, but justice it must be." Eleen looked at her King and then at the two Bishops, both seemed to quail under her stern gaze. The first stumbled out the word they needed "Death, yes DEATH" The second now feeling braver shouted his consent "DEATH." The King smiled young Eleen had played her part well without even knowing he saw her return the sword to the Lord.

THE KING SPOKE, "Take these two traitors from our sight and hang them from the bridge over the river and leave them for the crows to feed on." The two men did not have the strength or the will to resist and were dragged easily away. The Lords, Bishops, and people settled down once more the King sat and waited for the chatter to quieten. Oswi and Eleen stood apart from the Lords and warriors wondering what else would be happening. Eventually, the Lords went silent and waited for the King.

Once more the King stood looking down on his assembled people, none had seen him embroiled in a heated debate with the two Bishops moments earlier, but both now seemed subdued. The King raised his hands and spoke. "My Lords, the second issue we have been discussing these past days must now also be finalised, our two Lord Bishops have decreed to abide by my decision, I now require your own decisions"

Oswi and Eleen stood watching and listening they had no idea of what the King now spoke of.

The Old Lord whose sword Eleen had stolen slowly shuffled forward smiling at Eleen and nodding to Oswi he spoke as loud as he could for all to hear "I agree with our Lord Bishops and the King," He smiled, and continued as he looked once more upon Eleen "Who could not" Eleen was even more puzzled as one by one the Lords and Ealdormen stepped forward to agree only Ealdorman Alestan and Oswi's father had not responded, Ealdorman Ludeca spoke first "My Lord King and Lord Bishops, it is not right that I should answer," The bishop's looked at Ealdorman Ludeca and spoke "The King desires your answer Lord" Ealdorman Alestan laughed "We have to answer old friend" He looked to the King and bowed "I agree" now only Ealdorman Ludeca was left to respond he too looked upon his son and Eleen then to his King "I agree"

THE KING STOOD SMILING he had his victory, He looked down on Oswi and Eleen.

"Oswi, Eleen I as King of Mercia, and the Lords and Clergy of Mercia agree that you Eleen as a ward of the King you should marry" Eleen's heart sank. King Offa smiled and continued "Worry not Eleen, your suitor stands at your side if you are both in agreement with your peers"

Oswi looked at Eleen suddenly understanding that the King was allowing him to marry Eleen. Eleen too registered the Kings meaning and smiled looking at the King she bowed her head and said "I agree"

The King laughed as did all the Lords, Oswi's father grabbed Oswi pushing him towards his bride-to-be Eleen.

The King raised his hands once more and the Lords went quiet as he

spoke, "You are all aware of the actions that Thane Oswi has taken recently, the works here at Farndon, the rescue of Lady Eleen, and the battle against the combined forces of Powys, raiders, and Mercian traitors." The Lords all stood nodding in agreement Oswi stood holding the hand of Eleen as they listened to the King. The King smiled and looked down at Oswi and Eleen, "I have taken advice from our Bishops who kindly took up our invitation to attend, we have decided that from henceforth Thane Oswi will be Ealdorman Oswi of Holt, he will be charged with the defence of the river crossing and to keep our border safe here at Holt and Farndon." The assembled Lords and people all cheered.

Eleen stood surprised looking at Oswi, he would be her husband and would now be a Lord, he held her hand gently he too was surprised. The King descended the steps and gripped Oswi's arm "You are content, Lord Oswi?" Oswi smiled "Yes my King more than, I did not expect either reward." The King looked at Eleen, "You will care for her as if she was my own Oswi, I have not relinquished her as my ward and when you come to your wedding day I will give her to you" Oswi bowed his head "I understand Lord King" "Good, good. I have decided to leave a King's troop stationed here with you, I will provide new men to replace those lost, they can live and stable at Farndon under the command of the newly made Thane Ceoal who will hold Farndon under your command." Oswi made to reply but the King continued "Bern and his family can manage Crag Rock as we agreed and be your advisor, you will need fresh new guards, there are men here in Holt who are Mercian, some are former slaves who may be of use to you. I will leave you with some additional gold to assist you with rebuilding and employment of more guards for the future here at Holt.

Oswi looked at his King "My Thanks my Lord" he said slightly bowing his head.

The King Laughed "No Ealdorman Oswi, it is I that must thank you"

The two men stood a while before the King spoke once more " I will leave here in a few days' time though I will return in the spring for your marriage to Eleen." The King smiled "I feel we have a better future now Oswi, well done, very well done, but don't sit and relax our friend Healfden is still out there, watching and waiting, you need to stay alert."

The End

AUTHOR NOTES

I truly hope you have enjoyed my tale of Oswi, Bern, and Eleen. I hope to return to you next year with a new adventure for Oswi, in my second book "The Revenge." Which will follow the lives of Ealdorman Oswi & Lady Eleen and their companions.

The Betrayal was born from my love of reading and the work I have undertaken over the years doing advanced reviews & Beta reads for many authors. I provided some notes for an author friend and before I knew it I had decided to "Have a Go." I undertook research for the location of my book and the Kings of the eras.

I had in my mind a village by a river along the boundary of Mercia and Powys. Farndon is that place alongside the second village of Holt. (Which hundreds of years later) does have a Castle but not around the time when I drafted my own book, a bridge did stand over the river and the Romans were in the area though no main outpost or main Roman road. The Romans collected clay from the area around Farndon and the river banks of the Dee the nearest large Roman military base would have been modern-day Chester. I have

AUTHOR NOTES

always loved history and will be visiting the Wrexham/Holt area next year as we are on holiday nearby and intend to try and visit Offa's Dyke.

The only true character in my story is King Offa though the fights, action deeds, and timeline are fictious as are my characters and the events within my book. Oswi and his newfound fame and his loyal men will return to battle the raiders once more.

About the Author

I live in West Yorkshire with my wife Kirstie of 25 years (Who I would like to thank for supporting this venture) and our two grown-up sons. We have a cheeky little West Highland White her name is Trixy (and yes it fits her well)

Before Covid, we moved house to a semi-rural location best thing we did, we had nice walks to undertake during Covid.

I work for my local authority on recycling & waste and previously worked on local/national elections where I obtained qualifications in Electoral Law & Administration. I am a former Vice-Chair of a school governing body.

From a young age I had a great interest in reading back then it was David Eddings and Gemmal who grabbed my attention.

Through my early adulthood, I moved to Bernard Cornwell and Simon Scarrow. Then the last 5 years I found a new interest in reading and found some wonderful authors and started doing advanced review work and Beta reads for:

EM Powell, MJ Porter, CR May, SA Mckay, Adam Lofthouse, Stuart Rudge, Rob Samborn, Jemahl Evans, Tom Williams, Paula Lofting, Sam Taw, and various others. My love of reading has brought me a wealth of authors whom I love to support, I have accounts on Netgalley, Twitter, Goodreads, Amazon, Blog's on WordPress. I can be found by my name on all these accounts.

I decided to take that huge leap and try my hand at writing, I took advice and support from a wonderful lady and author whose work inspired me to write MJ Porter and her wonderful books, "The tales of Mercia series" and "Eagle of Mercia Chronicles." You can find more information on her website https://www.mjporterauthor.com/

ACKNOWLEDGMENTS

Every author has people he needs to say Thanks to I am no different. I started to draft my book in February 2022.

My wife Kirstie, though as she will confess is no reader, supported me and encouraged me to carry on. She has sat patiently, listened to me telling her about my book and how far I had got, and my plans for future chapters. Was there when I hit the wall and struggled to continue. I would not have committed to finish it without her support.

I was nearly half way through drafting my book before I actually felt confident to inform other family and friends. My immediate colleagues PH & JG encouraged me to continue. My parents read the first ten chapters of my initial write. I was on a roll, when they said they liked it. A colleague DB spent time doing a proof read for me and gave me some wonderful positive feedback for which I am very grateful.

Author MJ Porter has provided advice emails, messages, and chats for me as a new author on structure, editing as well as formatting and publishing along with advice on book covers, styles, and fonts, for which I will be forever grateful. MJ Porter also read the first few chapters and her feedback/advice helped me greatly moving forward with the book. MJ Porter was also on hand when I started to struggle to keep motivated.

Author SA Mckay read my 1st chapters and provided some great feedback and points/ideas.

And finally to you the readers. I hope you enjoyed the book. I will return with book 2 "The Revenge" please feel free to look me up on Twitter "Stacy Townend"

THE REVENGE

The Memory

Rain came as two sleek dragon-headed boats edged along the coast. A small wind gently carried them North, leaving the warriors to sit idly on the rowing benches. The sky had long since lost the glow of the sun and darkness enveloped the boats like a thick heavy blanket.

    The captain of the boat, Orm, stood, his rough hands holding the steering arm, he could barely see the shape of his Jarl stood leaning on the dragon-headed prow, and he could not see the sister ship behind and to his left, he just hoped that they still followed. The Jarl of the two fighting ships had positioned himself one foot on the rail and a hand on the dragon's head, staring out into the darkness, looking for the small cove that held the small fishing village that they were hoping to raid that night. Jarl Healfden stood, a dark cloak over his armour and a dark patch over one eye, further scars on his hands and face highlighting the brutal life he had endured. His face had a grim look and anger seemed to dwell in his eyes, he was quick to respond harshly to his warriors and the men who served him, a

THE REVENGE

few had even felt his sword take their lives. Healfden was a bitter and hard man, though he still drew men to follow him, as he shared his wealth and all prospered. He had fled the failed attack on Farndon with only ten of his father's followers remaining, now he commanded four ships and crews and had other new warriors to guard the settlement he could call upon a warband of around one hundred men, should he need to.

Tonight, he had two crews of around forty brutal and fierce warriors to attack the settlement. He had heard a trading vessel from further north had become stranded after the wild storm. Healfden decided the spoils of the trader should belong to him and his band of followers. He constantly attacked along this coast, and this would be the latest. It should prove to be fruitful, as it was rumoured the boat had slaves, wine, and oil in plentiful supply. Healfden looked around in the darkness. For some reason, he was reminded of his father when they had sailed up the River Dee to attack the settlement in support of

some Mercian traitors. He stood shocked as the flood of dark depressing memories of his father's demise and disorganised retreat smashed into him like a malicious spirit, grabbing hold of his heart and mind. Healfden was drained emotionally in an instant, as the memories flooded every sense. He stood and gave into them all remembering the details and events of the retreat one person's name on his lips "Berg."

Orm moved the small craft along the river, away from the village of Farndon, Looking around the craft at the few men trying to escape. Their Jarl was dead and lying at the edge of the village, nearly two ship's crews lay dead inside the village, on the rock path, or near the Old Roman bridge. The Jarl's son Healfden sat at the prow of the boat in silence, his head in his hands, the steadfast and loyal Berg behind him. Frode, a captain of the deceased Jarl Bjorn, lay next to Berg a deep gash along his head. Arn and Bo, two other friends of

Healfden sat next to him, both with sliced legs and arms from the hard fighting. Berg's older brother Rune was curled in a heap in the belly of the craft with a deep cut to his leg. The few others aboard the craft all had cuts and slashes to their hands, faces, and legs, not one free of injury.

Orm sighed as he let the river's current carry the craft away from Farndon. Berg had a cut above his eye and had lost two fingers on his left hand. He could not believe the combined forces of Raiders, Men of both Powys and Mercia had failed to capture the village. They had lost a whole ship's crew under Captain Renkel, who had been tasked to attack the watchtower. Renkel had sent men to guard the boats at the river while he attacked the tower. The Jarl had deemed it a secondary attack, Renkel was supposed to pin the stationed men down to ensure they didn't attack the rest of Jarl Bjorn's men from the rear. The idiot had instead been determined to wipe the group out at the tower. But had suffered huge casualties from the spears, rocks, and arrows that rained down on his men from the high vantage point of the tower. The defenders managed to barricade the bridge, pinning the survivors of the failed attack. More would have escaped but for Renkel. At least the idiot had died too.

Orm had been standing behind Jarl Bjorn when he had taken the fatal blow, Frode positioned

to his right and was also wounded. Gorm, the remaining captain of Bjorn, had been fatally injured and left dying inside the walled village, along with a good second ship's crew of men. They could not afford to lose so many. Orm felt the boat bump gently against the riverbank as he looked at the group of shattered survivors.

"Berg, push the prow off the bank, would you? We will let the current carry us further downstream before we trek to Wrexham."

Berg grabbed a spear and pushed the boat into the river, turning he spoke to Orm,

"The lads will not be able to walk far Orm, we need to get as far downstream as we can,"

THE REVENGE

Orm grunted a reply and watched as Berg laid a hand on the shoulder of his friend Healfden. The remaining men at Wrexham and The Valley stronghold would need to vote and decide if they would allow Healfden to lead them, he did a quick count of the men he knew they had left behind, roughly thirty in total, just over a decent ship's crew, not many at all. They had lost men when they had attacked King Offa and now the number had been decimated whilst attacking the village, fatal mistakes by, the now-dead, Bjorn. Orm had sailed many years for Bjorn and his father before him. He decided when he returned the remaining men to their homes he would fight and battle no longer for the Jarl's.

Orm had a wife and two grown sons at a small farmstead near Wrexham, he also had a small trading vessel that could be easily managed by a crew of eight. He would become a trader and live out the rest of his life in peace. Berg squeezed the shoulder of his lifelong friend Healfden, he had brutally lost his father Jarl Bjorn in the battle. Berg was only too aware they had lost too many men, and they may go seeking a new Jarl if Healfden could not assure the survival of them all through the coming winter. Berg would stay with him, for he was a true friend, and he hoped Arn, Bo, and his own brother Rune would too. Berg was sure Frode, once recovered, would stand by Healfden, but of the others he was unsure. He was aware Orm had seen more than enough action and wished to leave to stay alive.

Frode lay behind Healfden, his head pounding, he felt sick and dizzy and had vomited a few times, which made his head ache even more. A rough piece of cloth was wrapped around his head to try to stem the worst of the bleeding from the deep gash, lying across the full length of his brow. Frode had been stood alongside his old friend Bjorn, fighting the warriors of Farndon inside the very walls of the village. He could not believe they had fought so hard and bravely. They managed to defeat the combined attack from the Jarl's men, Chief Bledri's, and the group of traitorous Mercians. The retreat had

THE REVENGE

turned into a flood of desperate men once Jarl Bjorn had fallen and died. Frode had bent to help his Jarl when the young Mercian had leaped into attack him, swinging his sword at his neck, Frode had ducked out of the way but still the sword bit deep and long into his brow As he had fallen to his knees as Orm had stabbed, taking the young warrior in the throat, then quickly pulled Frode back into the second line. Berg sighed; he was unsure how this would all end. It could be the end of them, Healfden still needed to return to Wrexham and then onwards to The Valley to inform his mother of his father's demise.

In the bottom of the cold and leaking boat lay Frode. His head felt like a horse was continually kicking him. This along with the rocking of the boat had him feeling constantly sick. The cut along his brow was deep, and his head though wrapped up still bled down his nose and cheek into his beard, leaving him feeling as weak as a newborn baby. He had not the strength to speak with Healfden about his father Bjorn's death. He has been the oldest friend of Bjorn. Frode sighed, at least Bjorn died how he would have wished, by battling an enemy sword with axe in hand, his friends, and warriors beside him. Frode lifted his head to watch Berg, who was stood by his young Jarl's side, he was a good warrior with an exceptional inner calm and knowledge. It was strange but for want of birth Healfden and Berg could swap roles. Frode was now the only man alive to know the true father of Berg. It was not Colm as Berg believed, who had died in battle before his birth, but Bjorn. He was half-brother to Healfden and the better man, leader, and warrior. Frode knew he must keep his promise to Bjorn and not unveil the truth of it. Berg's mother Ethel, who died in childbirth, was a Mercian slave, abused time and time again, then given to Colm as a gift when falling pregnant. Rune Berg's older brother was also a child of Ethel, although his father nobody knew, as she had been raped so many times before becoming Bjorn's bed mate. Frode was ashamed, as he knew it was possible that he himself could hold the position of father to Rune. It was from that day he raped no more. It had sickened him to his very core. Frode fell asleep as he watched Berg and Healfden. Trouble could well be ahead if Frode was mistaken, and others knew of Berg's actual father.

Dark, shadowy figures stalked the small boat along the Powy's river bank. The raiders, so injured and despondent, never noticed them. Four figures clung to the trees and shrubs as they followed the small boat. Three children, the eldest a young lad of sixteen summers old, with his siblings another boy of twelve and his sister only eight years old. The only adult was a young warrior Euron, who had been left to look after the three children. The children Afan, Berwyn, and Alswn's father was the Bledri the tribal Chief of Holt. Euron himself was the younger son of Rathan the dead champion of Holt who also lay dead with Bledri. Holt and its surrounding lands and settlements now belonged to King Offa of Mercia. Euron and the three siblings were tired from the journey. Young Alswn slipped, knocking stones that tumbled down the river bank to loudly splash into the flowing river. The four froze as Orm and Berg turned weapons held ready and shouted to the area the noise had seemed to come from.

"Show yourselves, who is out there on the bank?" Euron looked to the youngsters before stepping from the deep dark shadows to call out a response. "I am a warrior of Bledri, son of his champion Rathan I am known as Euron Ap Rathan." Euron slowly and carefully rose proud and tall, a spear in one hand and a small hand of the shaking and terrified Alswn in the other. Afan and Berwyn the two sons of the deceased Bledri were at Euron's right. A short sharp sword in the hand of Afan and a seax gripped firmly in the smaller hand of Berwyn. The two warriors looked at each other in surprise. Orm shrugged his shoulders at Berg and nodded his head towards Healfden still poised and unmoving at the prow of the ship. The hand of Berg gently touched the shoulder of Healfden as he spoke softly in his ear. "Lord, surviving children of the dead Welsh Chieftain, should we offer assistance to them?" He did not respond slowly turning his head to look at the four shivering figures on the river side. "Bring them, they may have a use if we have further dealings with this man of Powy's." Berg simply nodded returning to Orm they waved them on board seating them on a bench near the steering arm.

Look out for "The Revenge" hopefully during 2023

Printed in Great Britain
by Amazon